RALEIGH REVIEW
LITERARY & ARTS MAGAZINE

VOL. 15.1
SPRING 2025

RALEIGH REVIEW

VOL. 15.1 SPRING 2025

PUBLISHER
Rob Greene

EDITOR-IN-CHIEF
Landon Houle

FICTION EDITOR
Jessica Pitchford

POETRY EDITOR
Chelsea Harlan, Samuel Piccone

ADVISORY POETRY EDITOR
D. Eric Parkison,
Leah Poole Osowski

EDITORIAL STAFF / FICTION
Dailihana Alfonseca, Alex Bryan,
Chas Carey, Madison Cyr,
Kelly McCorkendale,
Robert McCready,
Jeff McLaughlin,
Allison Frase Reavis

BOARD OF DIRECTORS
Joseph Millar, Chairman
Dorianne Laux, Vice Chair
Landon Houle, Member
Bryce Emley, Member
Will Badger, Member
Tyree Daye, Member
Rob Greene, Member

ASSISTANT FICTION EDITORS
Erin Osborne, Shel Senai

SENIOR COPYEDITOR
Elaina Ellis

COPYEDITOR
Charlene Pierce

EDITORIAL STAFF / POETRY
Erika Kielsgard, Heather Lang-Cassera,
Marty Saunders, Melanie Tafejian

SOCIAL MEDIA COORDINATOR
Maggie Busch

ILLUSTRATOR
Nora Beers Kelly

LAYOUT & PAGE DESIGN
Alexis Olson

LITERARY PUBLISHING PROGRAM
Alexander Gast

Raleigh Review, Vol. 15, No. 1, Spring 2025
Copyright © 2025 by *Raleigh Review*

Raleigh Review founded as *RIG Poetry*
February 21, 2010 | Robert Ian Greene

Cover collages by Geri DiGiorno
Cover design by Alexis Olson

ISBN: 978-1-59498-184-5

Distributed by Fernwood Press, an imprint of Barclay Press, Newberg, OR

Raleigh Review, PO Box 6725, Raleigh, NC 27628
Visit: raleighreview.org

RALEIGH REVIEW

table of contents

poetry cont.

RALEIGH REVIEW

VOL. 15.1 SPRING 2025

BREANNA GROW

WINTER SMELL

It's May, and every week a new flower blooms. You see it maybe a handful of times, stop and smell it twice if you're doing a good job of being present in the world, and then it's turning brown and falling over, so now every new flower makes you feel like that cartoon where the baby is wandering through a construction site completely unaware of the steel beam swinging its way. I could breathe in every last bud and still wouldn't really remember until next year when I realize I've been smelling hyacinths for decades, moments adding up to perhaps five minutes. I spend longer than that spacing out on the toilet every day. My Mom called again, and I ignored it this time because I already spent the morning waiting for her to tell me what the CAT Scan found, and it turned out the nurse wasn't actually saying "abnormalities" as code for "you've got stage 4 lung cancer," and I can't go back and forth like that between preparing to love her the very best I can in the time she has left and pretending I can always call her back. I mostly say I don't like winter, but at least you've got nothing to lose when you wake up expecting the sky and the ground to look the same, and then you get some chickadees and a cardinal in a pine tree, and you feel pretty lucky. I read somewhere that winter has its own smell, and someday it won't anymore. Will I miss it if I can't say what it was?

KRISTIN EMANUEL

IN WHICH THREE MICE INVITE ME TO TEATIME OR OBLIVION

i named my brother's lab mice as he infected them
with zika, ebola, coronavirus,
watched them die
on an excel spreadsheet—well,
at least they weren't anonymous:
she was rhododendron or marigold or beatrice;

i adopt my own mice & hold them every night
like palmfuls of light; they might

have been snakefood in another life—

instead they have me,
each other, their spats & routines.

for years, i watch them taper
until all three are buried:

one with a candy cane,
one with a marble,
the last with a glass figurine.

KIMBERLY SUAZO
THE ALIEN

HER NEW HOUSE had been advertised as having a lake view. She soon discovered it wasn't a lake but more of a half-empty hole, which she generously referred to as a pond. On days when the heat was bearable, she'd crawl out and go for a walk. She'd sometimes see a ripple on the pond's surface and wonder at the life that could survive the boiling water.

One day, standing by the pond, she saw a combine harvester drive by, a huge, slow monstrosity taller than her house. It was the first time she'd ever seen one up close. With her hand as a visor, she tried but failed to see the driver. She watched it move inch by inch and wondered if the air was cooler up there in the cabin. The next day, the vast expanse of green surrounding the hole was now a barren patch of brown. She didn't understand these farms. She never saw anyone working them. They were so different from the farms she knew, with rich, lush orchards ripe with

3

fruits and vegetables that demanded to be plucked, where the soil was fertilized by the nearby rivers and springs. She doubted the half-empty hole fertilized this dirt.

God, she missed the city. At least there she had the ocean singing its ancient song, the lyrics of which she recognized in her blood. Here there were no oceans, not unless you count seas of grasses and corn fields. Her own body recoiled from them, throwing tantrums at the weeds and dust in the air via incessant allergies that, to her horror, became a year-round affliction.

At home, she often stood in front of the mirror. She wiped the grime off her face and searched it. She smiled. She stopped. She inspected the fleshy pink of her lid. She let it go. She lifted her droopy breasts. She let them drop. When she wasn't in front of the mirror, she looked at her baby. It's all in you, she thought one day. Every last little drop I had managed to salvage, you now have. She stopped looking after that.

She sometimes pretended she was on another planet, one where the sun was further and kinder. At sunset, she blinked at the pink orb, completely unobstructed, and it smiled, looking her right in the eye as it said goodnight. She would keep up the pretense when she went to Walmart. She pushed the shopping cart, conjuring a sense of awe and discovery at the new species she found herself surrounded with. She took to naming them like an astronaut on a mission that must be documented. There's the *triple-fupasaurus*, rarely seen in the wild but who could sometimes be found lurking by the deli, slowly driving its electric cart. There's the *soccermaia*, commonly found in the dairy aisle with a pack of sandy-haired offspring trailing behind. There's the *clerkaravus*, always seen by the self-checkout stations handing out stickers and bad dad jokes. She smiled at them, grateful she didn't land on a planet with fauna as hostile as its terrain.

Her husband, it seemed, had gone native. He easily learned the language. He drank pop, played cornhole, and raved at the convenience of drive-thru fast-food joints. He'd make the locals holler at his funny stories about Earth. She half expected him to drive up in a double-cabin pickup truck and invite her to tailgate. It only made her feel more alien, other. More so than when the natives obsessed about her baby's caramel skin and curly hair.

He tried to help her assimilate. His latest attempt was a dinner date at the newest restaurant in town. As she sat there waiting for the pizza, she allowed herself to look. She looked at the beige walls, the brown floors, and the taped Out of Order sign over the A&W tap on the soda machine. When the pizza finally arrived and she bit into the soggy crust, she wasn't surprised, just disappointed. A disappointment that went down to her bones, rotting them from within. How could this be her new life, where all colors are a shade of dirt, and school cafeteria pizza is the hot

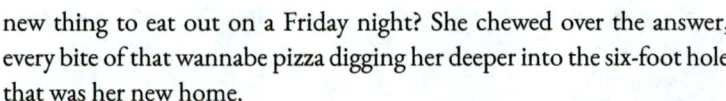

new thing to eat out on a Friday night? She chewed over the answer, every bite of that wannabe pizza digging her deeper into the six-foot hole that was her new home.

Staring at the full moon, she sometimes felt like she was back on Earth. The night sky, full of bright stars visible even with the moon's light, felt immense. So immense that she knew it was big enough to reach her old life. The same night sky she used to look up to before the hole and the dirt.

There were other fleeting moments of her previous life, like when she swung in the playground, the sharp smell of the metal chain under her nose. She would go as far up as possible, the gravitational pull making her stomach buzz. It was a feeling she craved. Sometimes she pondered, what if I jump?

She rode her bike as fast as she could, relishing the whistle in her ears and the cool breeze under her arms. Her t-shirt billowed and flapped behind her like wings. She closed her eyes, pedaled two rotations, and opened them again. Nope, still here, she thought.

The next time she rode, she closed her eyes, pedaled four rotations, and opened them again. She was still here. The more she rode, the longer she went, feeling closer each time. She took her bike out again and again, ten, twenty, thirty rotations. She was still here. The magic number was thirty-six, when with a jerk, she lifted out of her seat, and for one precious moment, she felt she had done it, that she had finally taken off. ◆

STEVE NICKMAN

THE PAPERWEIGHT

An elegant brass hand, maybe a woman's,
with long, slender fingers, a ring on the fourth,
that holds a shining ball.
My patients ask me what it is.
A door-knocker, I say,
from a house I used to live in.
They hold it, feel its heft,
notice the hole beneath the wrist
where it was attached.

I stole it
after my parents' house was sold,
in broad daylight, too.
And years before, when I was five,
I took the metal letter D
that hung loose from a nail
outside a flower shop on Broadway.
Later it still said ORCHIDS
with the D in a different font.

In college, a little book
of medieval poetry
with glorious colored illustrations
spoke to me from a shelf in the student lounge.
And there were darker things.
My young visitors don't need to know
that part of me.
I keep my dark in the polished ball
contained within the hand.
I'm not alarmed
by anything they say.

KEVIN THOMASON

ZERO SPEAKS

It's not that I'm nothing, no,
just the nothing that blunders
beyond—stomach on a stick figure,
gap of a missed zipper,
quickie she wished had been quicker.

All the integers abut but me.
Unrehearsable number
going on at once. Where I'm from,
I'm the nothing that nothing entertains,
the cosmic rattling of shit for brains.

Find me in rings that ride out
to calmness on a lake face.
But I'm the plunk of the rock
that struck it, the butt-head, the bore,
punk ass mooning you from the shore.

NATHAN ALLING LONG

THE INTERNATIONAL SPACE STATION KNOWS HOW I FEEL

LAST YEAR, my partner of eight years took a job 250 miles to the north. We now drive five hours up and down to spend long weekends together, trying to hold together a relationship that had already shown signs of disintegrating. On one trip, he showed me the tiny house he'd just bought, which sits a block from Lake Ontario. From the upstairs bedroom, he pointed out the endless blue field of water.

The International Space Station is the same distance, hovering 250 miles above the Earth. It's composed of two modules, American and Russian, each of completely different designs. They're foreign to each other, except for the coupling that fits them together.

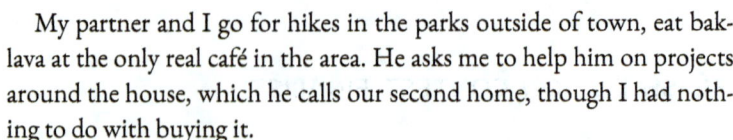

My partner and I go for hikes in the parks outside of town, eat baklava at the only real café in the area. He asks me to help him on projects around the house, which he calls our second home, though I had nothing to do with buying it.

When I was twelve, I bought a whole sheet of US stamps that commemorated the Apollo–Soyuz docking. It was the first manned international space mission. I dreamed of being on it, up high, above my life. I imagined the Earth, a bright blue ball spinning slowly against the black field of space. I thought for sure that union in space would end the Cold War, the endless nuclear arms.

Sometimes my partner and I take kayaks on the Great Lake, along the shore, where the waves are calmer. When we're tired, we pull our boats up, side by side, and lay the oars across both boats, so they become one object. We eat sandwiches as we drift on the water, the sky above us as large and peaceful as the lake.

When I think of the space station now, all I can imagine are the dangers—exposure to radiation, the chance a life support system will break down, and the failure of shuttles to rescue the astronauts. Mostly, I imagine all those hours floating through the emptiness, feeling unconnected to anything, even though one module is attached to the other.

Sometimes when I'm up there, 250 miles north, spending those days in my partner's tiny house, I become adrift. I feel a pull to get in my car and drive home. Other times I don't want to leave, don't want to return to that empty house we once shared.

For the astronauts on board, there's so little gravity, their bones and joints begin to loosen, their bodies slowly pulling apart. There's also the constant pull of Earth, tugging at the station and the crew like a thought. *Come back down, come back home.*

It's easy to skip a weekend—we get busy or simply want to avoid the ten hours of driving. Then a half month has passed before we see each

other. When we meet again, my partner seems a different person, his skin darker, his hair longer. He's met new friends who he talks about as he cooks me dinner.

The station is turning twenty-five years old this year. Things are already breaking down. It's not supposed to last past 2024.

Last week, I drove up to help my partner repair the soffit on his roof. I held the ladder, passed things up, and talked about work between the poundings of the hammer. He paused at times and told me what he saw, over the pitch of the roof—the waves of Lake Ontario crashing against the breakers, the sailboats with their colored sails, an oil tanker far out in the water. But sometimes I couldn't hear him, his words drifting off the roof toward the lake.

They always have two of the astronauts walk out of the station into space together. They never let one be exposed to all the elements, to the vast void, alone. The way it works, one repairs some damage while the other remains tethered to him, to make sure he doesn't get frightened or lonely, or simply float away. ◆

KATHERINE BARRETT SWETT

LOST LANGUAGES

So many languages have fallen
off of the end of the world
> —Lucille Clifton, from "here yet be dragons"

It is a fairy tale in reverse, a deresurrection,
an unimaginable unimagining of our tongues.

It happens through encounters and through willful destruction
suddenly or gradually. When do we know that what we knew

will never return, that the barrier
of bison is gone forever,

that eventually there could be one speaker left of your village dialect
that was language to you? Beads without strings, syntax forgotten,
the sound you loved

that started from the back of the throat and spilled through the lips.
Think of all the forgotten poems and the forgotten

children, the human encounters that exist unrecorded,
the horrors, the tenderness,
the unsewing of language, unimaginable words without referents,

like those birds exploding at dawn, all gone. A million worlds gone
and what did the cat say when he scratched my leg?

LAUREN CAMP

NOMINAL OUTER LIMIT OF KNOWLEDGE

Disheveled light enters the house and ravens
pick up the battle
of daybreak; the roof climbs to
a seam and falls
toward the quarter
out west. Voyaging, leaping
wind eating itself. Everything is
waiting not to be
wind. The day sleeves on
and we decide to turn
a direction. At a museum we lift
levered cams and stir
the small blue tooth
of a wheel. We are now
in a glorious break from the turbulence.
Instead, a summer day with a little
centrifugal force and kinder
time-lag and
helix. And then we revel
in the back
gallery with its thirteen
definitions of the portrait of Lisa
Gherardini, wife
of Francesco, and her infinite
delicate mouth. Her quiet is
bedlam in infrared
visions. We hardly notice the baluster,
parapet, and butterfly
spline on 15th century poplar.
From the edges of that sandy
flesh, we can measure eternity.

Then walk straight out,
air again cresting a curve. It goes on
with its infinite target
but I no longer believe it.

ANGELA TOWNSEND

POLL DANCING

IT WAS NEVER about pocket money. Glad as I am to earn a Wawa gift card or fluff my PayPal pillow, I would take consumer opinion polls for free.

It started in college. While my fellow anthropology majors shot tequila and mapped each other's freckles, I exercised the full powers of introversion in the computer lab.

Three stations down, Arnold excavated a young eBay for science fiction memorabilia. Arnold was precocious. He started college at sixteen and was already ahead of schedule for becoming a senior citizen. He wore beady turtlenecks and asked if he looked like Woody Allen. He brought his own shaker of Old Bay seasoning to the dining hall.

In the computer lab, Arnold chewed Werther's caramels and expelled a soft "heck yeah!" several times an hour. He interrupted me to share knock-off Spocks and to ask what I was answering.

More often than not, I was evaluating paper towels. The survey over-lords asked if I would trade softness for strength. They presented me crop circles of perforation patterns, demanding which looked most ab-sorbent. I devoted hours of the least wrinkled years of my life to consid-ering select-a-size sheets. I made tens of cents an hour.

Occasionally, the opinion polls overplayed their hand. Twelve pages into an inquest on toaster pastry, questions could take a hazardous turn. "How often do you feel you are no good at all?" "How many occasions in the last thirty days have you been unable to stop worrying?"

Arnold found this electrifying. "They want to know if people high in neuroticism prefer unfrosted Pop-Tarts! Someone is paying for this!" He joined my panel, and I received a bonus of one dollar for the referral.

But Arnold abused the system. "I'm going to tell them that I am Poly-nesian and ninety-nine years old!"

"Don't do that. You'll mess up the research."

"You really care about the research?"

Having no experience in even entry-level hooliganism, the fun-sized valedictorian lacked stamina. I heard a Werther's shatter between his teeth the night he was busted. "Oh, no!"

"What?"

"They're kicking me off the panel." His apricot cheeks bleached. "My answers are inconsistent with sincere participation."

"That's what you get for telling them you're a geriatric hula boy."

"I also told them I like my paper towels two feet long and printed in Elvish."

Arnold's eyes searched mine for absolution, but the corners of his mouth started twitching. Soon, the boy who did not look anything like Woody Allen laughed harder than the night he'd dared me to justify my preferred brand of toilet paper, "the force is strong with this one."

I receive unmarked rolls of Bounty every few Christmases, so I know Arnold is out there mostly behaving himself. I hope he has assembled a complete set of every Boba Fett ever committed to plastic. I hope he found a girl who was not too neurotic to realize he liked her.

Meanwhile, I am still taking surveys. Household paper products remain the dominant topic. There is no more urgent inquiry than the longings left unrequited by wiping the counter.

If the surveyors ever stare back through my webcam and ask why I answer, I am not sure I could tell them.

It is a peaceful hobby, though I sometimes tire of rehearsing my demographics. When I am the precise "peculiar" a survey seeks, there is real money. I once earned twenty dollars from a panel trawling for left-handed Enneagram 2's who use continuous glucose monitors and have never tasted Beaujolais. (I screened out of a follow-up poll because I do not use dryer sheets.)

But I am beginning to understand Arnold's treachery. While I am placidly passing my time, unseen deciders with shiny foreheads commit my profile to ink. To them, I am a divorcee who prefers corn-based kitty litter. I consume precisely the volume of Greek yogurt expected for my gross income and body mass index. I display average openness to new experiences and a level of neuroticism worthy of a documentary and a lifetime supply of emotional support Pop-Tarts. I stockpile enough paper towels to mummify myself. They are all select-a-size.

I am ready for new questions.

I want someone to ask if I think the repugnant Charmin bears are proof of several Freudian constructs and the imminent apocalypse. Inadequate inquiry has been devoted to the moment I realized I would turn forty-five before my Spaghetti-O's expire. I am still waiting for someone to question why I feel safe every time I see a cat tuck her nose under her tail.

I would tell them I believe we are all born quilted, though we forget.

I would tell them I may be forty-three (as they all know), but some people think I can pass for forty-two. I will be happy to answer follow-up questions about eye cream.

I would tell them it is harder to make people laugh than cry, and they should always include a question about hula dancing or Doritos after asking if I sometimes feel no good at all. ◆

EMILY WITHENBURY

WINDOW BETWEEN

	Somehow,
I've never been held like this.	
Echo in your eyes I can't quite	
place. It's home &	distance.
Soft forehead against mine	
as we break open	in this town of
umbrellas. Inside, a diner	
counter curved, contained.	Beyond
my face, your hands—steady	
rain sheens down	the pane.

BETSY JOHNSON

I'M SO GLAD I'VE BEEN LOST

with the discarded angels the snake skin in the park

the stub of a candle in a cave my tumor in

the garbage can i've heard death

is nothing more than a moving from one breast

of god

to the other the glory of a new

fullness slake slake this thirst i beg you

pull me close but not too soon from the familiar even if

even when the familiar

heaves, shrivels

J. DOMINIC PATACSIL

LITTLE BATTLES

IT'S THE LITTLE THINGS that remind me I'm an idiot, like when my co-worker dies and I think to text Gemma. Doyle sat at the cubicle over from me for four years, and I want to tell Gemma that a drunk driver smashed him plum into the ravine. We only just heard about it. The boss man came in with consternation and pity wrapped up in his cheeks to tell us that we'd send company flowers.

Everyone is on their phones, calling husbands and wives and mistresses and pets while I sit and look at that empty cubicle. I think that Doyle probably ate more egg salad sandwiches in his shortened lifetime than I could ever achieve. I think Gemma might find that interesting. She might pose the question as to whether or not I thought Doyle made his egg salad special or if he just bought it from the store. I'd say that if

I knew anything about accountants, Doyle had run the macros. Home-made was the way to go. I try to type the words, *My egg salad coworker died*, but stop halfway.

I'm reminded of a moment just before Gemma left me. We stood in the grocery checkout line. She was reading the tabloid headings aloud and got to *Carrie Demands Divorce After Sex Scandal* before she quit it.

How do we keep going? she asked me. *When does it ever work out?* I shrugged and asked her if she'd thought the grocery bill would be under a hundred dollars. She said it wouldn't be and looked disappointed.

I read the text I've started and consider what can come of it. All roads to Gemma are dead. There was a time when she loved me, when we en-joyed alternative Japanese films and competed to see who could get the sweatiest ass from the spin class we both used to attend. But those plea-sures ended when Gemma stepped away from me. She said she had to work on herself.

What can you do but applaud that? Saying *I can make it better* doesn't work. I've tried. But I want to make it better, and I want her to believe that I can, and I just don't want to be alone, like I am right now, thinking even if I sent a message to Gemma and she didn't respond, it would feel better than swallowing all these words.

Everyone else's conversations are wrapping around my head. I've heard the phrase *drunk driver* too many times today. So many times that I find myself staring at the sticky notes taped to Doyle's monitor, won-dering what he felt in the very last moment.

I have a nice thought that maybe he was at peace. Maybe he was look-ing into the ravine, which is green and flowery this time of year, unaware of the Ford pickup that had crossed the median. I pray this is true and start another text message to Gemma where I fib and say it is. But some-thing stops me from sending it.

Maybe it's that I know it isn't the truth. That it's fairly dishonorable to wax poetic when someone you know has died. Maybe it's that I know Doyle must've been screaming to high heavens or even calculating in fast math the probability that all of it was happening to him. On that road, at that time, in that spot, I put the odds at one in 6,500.

And this is my lowest. This is when I feel the idiot alive in me. I think to ask Gemma if she would take that line. I found it sexy how calculated her bets used to be—or are, I guess. Shit.

This wrecks me, the notion that there came a moment in Gemma's beautiful brain when I was no longer worth the risk.

And she can say it was to work on herself, but we both know she's shielding me from something. Something which I still can't bear to acknowledge because it will force me to forgo those sweet moments, like when we compared ass sweat in the gym mirror.

I am inadequate. I am inept. I am the cheese between your toes. How am I supposed to find my way back? I don't even know which way is up.

I have written this text at least a million times, and like the rest, I do not send it. I feel exposed by my words, by how weak I've become. Sending this will get me no closer to the feelings I try to pump with life. All roads to Gemma are dead.

I wish Doyle were here to tell me this. He had that calm and stupid way about him that could set anyone at ease.

I wonder what he's doing now. I wonder if the egg salad in heaven uses dill. I want to feel close to him.

I get up and walk a cubicle over. Nobody notices me. They are distracted by their conversations, which have drifted from the original purpose to dinner plans, to picking up the kids, to the lumber sale happening at Menards.

I sit in Doyle's chair. It's a swivel back, and I do a couple circles. I grab the desk to steady myself, but the brain inside me keeps going. It spins on and on, while I study the tidy quarters of Doyle's professional life: his Casio extra large, his cup of blue and black pens, those sticky notes taped to his monitor.

There are two of them. The first one reads, *Pass: M@rth4St3waRt!*. The second one reads, *You have never been weaker. You have never been stronger. You have only been here.*

I stand and try to make it seem that Doyle's desk has remained untouched, but I'm dizzy. My brain won't stop spinning. I have the thought that I am circling the drain.

I take the second sticky note and fold it into my pocket, then immediately remove it to read it again. There are three sentences. Declarative sentences. Sentences with little room for air. I read them, and I read them, and I start to think that these people around me, they talk awfully loud. ◆

PATRICK KINDIG

BE KIND TO ME I'M STRUGGLING

is what my brother titles
the first song he's written
since moving back
to michigan with
the woman we all
expected him
to marry because
they adopted two dogs
together & at christmas
she led the family
singalong full
of irish coffee
& good cheer but
now the two of them
have separated & my brother
is asking for kindness
in a song he has posted
on facebook which
he plays on an old piano
in an empty house
in detroit where
just six months ago
his dogs flounced
& floundered in
my lap as his girlfriend
repeated *down boys*
down & my glasses fell
to the floor before
i got on a plane & flew
back to texas where
my husband was waiting

where i am now
watching my brother
from 1,300 miles away
play piano & repeat
be kind to me be kind
to me & i want to
but i'm struggling
to know how
such kindness looks
separated as we are
by four states
& the mississippi
river which
during that last visit
my brother told me
he had never crossed
& I said *you guys*
have to come visit
& my brother nodded
& his girlfriend nodded
& the dogs played
at my feet on the floor
& my brother said *of course*

CARLIN CORSINO

GHOST COSTUME

The most realistic costume
is the ghost costume
with its wrinkled veil
that cuts a wearer
from the bolt of life's muslin
into the shape of a finger
which points accusingly at the sky
for leaving it behind. Like death
it reduces a child's laughter
to muffled echoes within a pale cave
and white noise of fabric
whispering down a hallway on certain days
when you least expected to be reminded
or a keepsake blanket which rustles
as it swaddles a doll grasped
from the memories drawer
placed back on a bedroom shelf
by grieving parents in that hush
as the eyes of the past
through their round lenses
now peer from closer by.

PATRICIA O'DONNELL
GRATITUDINE

ON THE CITY BUS to the hotel, Gwen identified the problem. She had forgotten to feel grateful. She was on vacation with her husband Jack, two weeks in Italy, and all she'd been able to think about was how tired she was, how much her feet hurt, how her allergies made her cough, and how her life was going in a wrong direction. A vacation in Italy, she'd thought, couldn't change the fact that she was heading for retirement, which would be fine except for the suspicion that most people at the tech company where she worked would be happy to see her go. It couldn't change the fact that her parents were dead and her daughter Ellie didn't need her anymore. Or that she would never again see men's heads turn toward her when she walked down the aisle in an airplane.

Gwen and Jack caught the bus outside the Venice airport. It was there, as she settled into the vinyl seat with her suitcase held between her knees, that she remembered to be grateful. What a wonderful opportunity this long-awaited trip was! How many people would be grateful to have this opportunity! She remembered, as the Italian sunshine fell through the tall windows of the bus, that she was grateful to be alive, and not only for this trip, but for her beating heart, her breathing lungs.

The feeling of relief spread through her as they got off the bus and walked through the city, rolling their suitcases behind them. *Grateful,* she thought. *I am grateful.*

After a few wrong turns down precipitously narrow alleys, they found their hotel—an ancient three-story house on a crowded street corner next to a canal. Looking up from the street, they saw arched windows and a balcony with window boxes overflowing with flowers. They pushed an intercom button, heard some incomprehensible Italian words to which Jack replied, "We have a reservation." And they were admitted to climb a narrow turning staircase with old carpeting on the steps.

At the top, they were greeted by a gnomish face under a thatch of dyed blonde hair. The woman took a metal key from the wall and showed them their room, speaking rapidly in Italian all the time. Gwen caught a word now and then, but Jack knew no Italian beyond *ciao* and *buono sera. Gratis,* the woman said, gesturing at the bottles in the mini refrigerator. She showed them how to close the heavy wooden blinds against the sun. *Grazie,* Gwen kept saying. *Grazie mille.*

When the woman was finally gone, they fell on the bed in relief. Gwen's laughter seemed to free something in Jack, and he was laughing too. Then they were fumbling with one another's clothes. They moved slowly with one another, gentle in the warm Italian air. The sun fell in thin strips across them through the wooden blinds. Jack's skin was loose and soft, like hers: well-known, familiar, though it had been a while since they'd made love. *Grateful,* Gwen thought. She was aware of music playing somewhere below them, a slow repetitive organ sound, meditative almost, with no voices. It was the background to their lovemaking. They kept their voices and sighs quiet, thinking of neighbors next door, of the woman down the hall.

Afterwards, they used the bidet. She showed Jack how. "No, turn around the other way." She opened the bottle of spumante from the refrigerator and took it and two glasses to the small balcony overlooking the street. She poured Jack a small glass, against his protests. "Here we are," she said. "We made it." A woman on the sidewalk below stood looking up at them. She carried a plastic cup of a pale liquid. Gwen raised her wine glass and called out, "Cheers! Sláinte!" The woman's face broke open in a smile and she raised her glass also. "Cheers!" she shouted up at them. Gwen poured herself another glass and drank. She felt revisited by happiness. A sense of openness, of possibility. All due to gratitude, and to Venice, and a little wine. She tried to pour more into Jack's cup.

"No!" he said, holding his hand over his cup.

"Come on," she said. "Celebrate with me."

He pulled the cup away and spoke sharply. "Just stop," he said. "I don't want anymore."

His tone cut her. She felt herself close against him, pull away. She didn't want to look at him or speak to him. He was a joy-killer, she thought. No wonder she'd been depressed.

That was married life. They put the remaining spumante back in the mini-fridge and left to find dinner, locking the door behind them. Gwen reached back in herself to find the note she'd found before. *Gratitude. Grateful.*

The woman who'd let them in was crouched down below the desk, reaching for something. When she stood up and saw them her face had changed; no longer smiling, she gave them a sour look. As if she didn't like them, in particular she didn't like her, Gwen. Had she overheard their sounds in the bedroom? Or was she fed up with entitled, self-obsessed Americans? "*Ciao,*" Jack said, and the woman mumbled something in reply.

In the street, the sun slid behind the buildings as late afternoon shifted to early evening. A family passed them, and with the sound of children's voices she felt a familiar pang: the memory of Ellie as a young child, the joy of that time. All gone, and with it her youth, the sense of possibility and joy that was just present, not needing to be analyzed or encouraged. She reached out to touch Jack's hand, and he took her hand in his. He squeezed her hand. She needed him. They needed one another.

They walked on cobblestones in the pedestrian street, stopping at a restaurant with tables outside under a striped awning. "How's this?" Jack asked. It looked like every other restaurant. The menu posted on a sign showed reasonable prices.

"Fine," she said. A waiter pulled out a chair, bowing. "Madam." She preferred the other chair, facing out, but thanked him. She felt the familiar tickle in her lungs and put her head down to the menu, trying to keep her coughs quiet. "Sorry," she said, wiping her mouth with the napkin.

The waiter pulled out his notepad with a flourish. "May I recommend," he said, pointing to the sea bass special. "For two. Very fresh. With vegetables."

They ordered the special without asking the price—it was Italy, how expensive could it be?—and glasses of wine. After that, they waited a long time. People next to them were seated, ate their pizza, left, and still they waited for their food. At last a cart was wheeled to their table. On it lay a massive bass, gaping at her. It looked disappointed: if it had to lose its life, it would have hoped to feed six people at least.

The waiter cut off its head and dropped it in a little bucket sitting on the cart. He cut down the fish's middle and pushed it open. Moving the knife around, he muttered. "No, no." The fish was pink inside. "Five more minutes," he said, and pushed the cart away from the table.

So close, so close. It had been a long day of traveling. While they waited she made conversation with Jack, forcing herself to be pleasant, to look at him. They were surrounded by other people; she didn't want them to look at this American couple sitting glumly. She didn't want them to dislike them or, worse, feel sorry for them. After a time, Jack waved at the man who seemed to be the manager and asked where their food was. Finally, finally, the tray was wheeled back to their table, and they were served. The fish was well cooked, but too much for them to eat. When the bill came, Jack's eyes opened wide. It was—Gwen calculated—fifteen times the price of the single sea bass dish listed on the menu.

She told Jack as they walked back that it wasn't just the money they spent; it was the feeling that they'd been made fools of. Identified as American tourists too naïve to ask the price of the special, so the price had been jacked up, even if it had taken an hour to be delivered. Jack was quiet, walking with his hands in his pockets. She'd wanted to complain to the manager, but Jack said no. He was slipping into the role of the adult, the one to calm his hysterical wife down. She wasn't hysterical, she told herself, just . . . just . . . travel was hard. *Gratitude*, she reminded herself, but the word felt hollow.

At the hotel, they let themselves in with the old metal keys they'd been given. The reception desk was empty, the lights low. In their room, Gwen lay on the bed, staring at the ceiling. The sea bass sat uncomfortably in her stomach, minus head and bones. The room was suffused with a sweet smell; insect repellent, she thought, which made her wonder what might be crawling around under the bed. *Gratitude,* she remembered, and for some reason felt the sting of tears. She closed her eyes to hide it. There was so much wrong with her life. Yet she knew she was lucky; she knew most people in the world would look on her with envy. Gratitude was a requirement. How did people with real problems—refugees, political prisoners, hostages, people with terminal diseases, people in a war zone—how did they survive? Where did they find their strength?

She undressed and brushed her teeth. In bed she kissed Jack on the forehead. His body was familiar, almost like her own. She pressed herself along his length, feeling his warmth. When people marry, the Bible says they become one flesh. She was as unhappy with Jack as she was with herself; she hated him and loved him like she hated and loved herself. He was part of her, and they were part of one another, one flesh like trees whose roots meet underground. "Good night," she said.

He kissed her back, on the lips. "Good night."

In the dark, she pulled the old satiny coverlet up to her chin. Soon Jack's breath became even and soft. He was asleep. She heard the organ sound again, from somewhere below her. A repetitive, almost monotone sound, slow and sad. It was the sound, she thought, of the old Venice, of the lives that used to live here when this hotel was a house, when the neighborhood was full of tradesmen and running children instead of tired, drunk tourists, when people fell in love here on this street corner and lingered on the bridge at sunset, stealing kisses. It was the music of those who had died here, whose spirits were part of the place like their bodies were. They stayed because they loved the lives they had lived so much.

She saw the woman's face from earlier grimacing at her and the waiter bowing at their table. She coughed, and coughed again. It occurred to her then with great clarity that her cough was not allergies at all, but something else. Something that would entwine its arms around her, pulling her into the earth to become a part of it, and a part of all the lives that would follow until they followed no more, until the earth was a brittle husk, the wind blowing across an arid planet. There was nothing to do but accept.

Gwen took a breath. She was not important. Just one of many bodies teeming and contesting in the daylight, curled up against one another for warmth at night. *Grateful,* she breathed, the word a bubble holding emptiness. But an emptiness that was beautiful like glass, or like a soap bubble, with shifting colors and shapes on its surface. Her life would not last forever, but was given to her to fight with, to love. She was so grateful. ◆

AUDREY HALL

UNFATHOMABLE

A child gawks under the humpback whale skeleton:
Humphrey, preserved in this museum gallery,
died on a Florida beach.

His jawbone hints at a Biblically cavernous gullet.
The chain-link of his vertebrae dwarfs
that of the mastodon below.

The boy's hands jolt up with open fingers
as though to grasp two ribs by their ends
and pull the mystery of the whale down to him.

THE CLEAVING

Around the tree of the world winds the amphisbaena,
peridot gazes minding the four directions.

Hanging on an iron pin, writhing forward and back,
it germinates the universe with blood limned in pollen.
Its scales wink at and warn humankind below.

This is how the world begins: the amphisbaena teething
at the fabric of a carob tree, end after end after end.

SCOTT POMFRET

HOW TO EXIT A TWENTY-YEAR GAY RELATIONSHIP

DEFINITELY NOT GRACEFULLY. Put aside that ambition. There's no soft landing.

Begin the process with a drunken post-dance-club blow-out during which you mutter the forbidden words "break up" to your boyfriend for the very first time. Wake the next morning full of regret. Sob together all day. Have make-up sex and dinner with friends. Pretend it never happened, even though those words can never be unsaid, and the concept's no longer inconceivable. It has a name.

Hear those magic words whispering through the beach grass: *Break-up. Break-up. Break-up.* Hear them amplified in every NPR newscast, no matter what the host may be talking about.

Begin to think: this might be a thing.

Start an endless series of Long Talks. They'll be circular and unpleasant, particularly as it dawns on your boyfriend what you're trying to say.

Use suffocating, patronizing rationality. Explain how people grow apart. Mention different goals in life. Mention that each of us needs to tend his own garden. Utter these platitudes even though the real reason for breaking up is something emotional and hard to rationalize, even to yourself.

Suffer the mutterings that you're having a midlife crisis. They'll come from your boyfriend. Your friends. Your mother. She'll say, "I put up with that bastard your father for fifty-three years, you think it was all wine and roses?" (For the record, you don't. You think she should have dumped his sorry ass.)

Endure the minefield of reminders of the good times, such as that sacred memory from your first year together, when you taught your boyfriend to drive a stick shift after you'd both consumed three-quarters of a bottle of Jose Cuervo and didn't kill anyone or yourselves in the process, as if God intended your relationship to last forever.

Seek professional help. Learn to use I-statements. Agree to list all the things you're going to do to save the relationship and all the reasons you've valued each other over these twenty years. Be thinking the entire time, 'I'm not sure I *want* to save the relationship.' Don't notice this is a problem until your boyfriend points out that your uncertainty makes you a particularly uncooperative participant in list generation.

Spend time apart. Seek allies. (You both will.) Avoid anyone who challenges your account of what happened. Avoid those who ask, "You're just going to throw it away after twenty years?" Avoid disputing words like "just" and "throw away" or even the agency the question implies.

Instead, blame plate tectonics. Forces that move slowly but cause earthquakes. Erosion. Pride yourself on geological metaphors and unflinching engagement with hard decision making.

Whatever you do, do *not* comparison shop to justify your decision. Don't let the fresh young face down the block catch your roving eye. It'll only give credence to the accusations of a midlife crisis. (And when you eventually do comparison shop, despite this good advice, don't act like it's a revelation from on high that fucking a total hot young stranger, no strings attached, is uncomplicated fun. Like bubblegum.)

Have doubts.

Have many, many doubts.

Sob privately. Rinse. Repeat.

When your boyfriend gives you a particular nostalgic pair of wooly socks for Christmas, sob some more. (He'll probably sob, too, if he's forgiven you for comparison shopping.)

Compose a birthday slideshow of the best pics of you two together over twenty years. Set it to *The Man I Love*. Don't be surprised that it ends up looking and sounding like one of those slideshows you play at a wake.

Split the assets. Divvy up the mutual friends. **Disappoint others. Fail to meet expectations, which are particularly acute because everyone holds you responsible for proving gay relationships are at least as real.**

Feel like you've crash landed. Tip back a shot of Cuervo for courage.

Tend your garden. Set your goals. Have Long Talks with yourself.

Sob publicly. Rinse. Repeat.

Blow yourself up on the memory minefield. Pick shrapnel from your brain. Listen to the wind whistling through the gaps: *broken up broken up broken up*.

Don't act surprised when your ex-boyfriend acquires a smarter, richer and more handsome partner than you ever were. Be kind to yourself. When you run into your ex-boyfriend and his new lover, as you inevitably will, because the gay community is too goddamn small, be kind to them, too. Don't suppose people are saying you got what you deserved (but they probably are).

Feel guilty over the first glimmers of relief that it's finally over. Find it harder to get a date now that you're not attached. Flex those withered flirtation muscles. Wish you could commiserate with your ex about all your tragic first dates. Of all people, he'd certainly understand. ◆

BRENDAN STERMER

TIMELAPSE

after Archibald MacLeish

—And here upon my childhood bed,
to stretch a limb and crack an eye,
to hear my mother's muffled tread
and wonder what she whisks and why,

and wonder if she whisks for me
or for the grieving neighbor girl,
and catch a whiff of rosemary,
and hear a gray metallic whirl

rise up above the softer sounds
of sliding drawer and cupboard creak,
and whispers of black pepper ground
into a broth of boiled leaks

—and then to see her bent in a bed
of berries, or picking a bunch
of basil for a sandwich spread,
perhaps for a late summer lunch

or dinner with the family,
at six o'clock, to hear them come,
to hear her sighing anxiously
and dashing to get dinner done,

then cue the hum of family news,
the slicing of large crusty loaves,
the friendly clashing of our views
on culture, or the neighbor's woes

—and late, to hear the kettle sound,
to hear her pouring midnight tea,
to hear her rummaging around
for yet another recipe . . .

and back again upon my bed,
to love that distant lullaby—
the sliding drawer, the muffled tread—
and wonder what she whisks and why.

VICTORIA JEAN REYNOLDS

I'M IN LOVE WITH LOT'S WIFE

when she hands me her homemade soppressata,
cured with the salt of her very own skin.

She jokes she's wasting away, the sleet
this morning at the market has dissolved

the soft slope of her shoulder, just outside
the black umbrella's range.

I don't know her name, so I cannot call
her when someone comes behind with a shovel,

pushing the salt of her out into the road.

IAN LINDSAY

NON-FUNGIBLE

OUTSIDE Jeff Dizon's kitchen window, alongside a lichen-crusted fence, loomed a swing set he couldn't take down. Florida sun bled off the chain links from where he sipped coffee over the sink. None of his family used the swings, not since Katie. Since it had happened, the peace was thin between Jeff and Carolyn. Arguments were stifled words. Polite cruelness. He loved his wife but knew that strain only lasted so long. Maybe until Anthony left? He wanted his son's flight off to college prolonged. Not just for his marriage.

Jeff rinsed his mug—grateful he'd taken a sick day at the tech firm where he worked in management. When the house emptied, he'd Zoom with his lawyer, Luisa Morse, and could avoid sitting through grueling traffic. Soon, Carolyn would drop Anthony off at Vista Point High, her agreed duty for the last three years. Jeff won't visit the school. Not anymore.

Road rage was his vice. Earlier that week, a lifted F-150 cut him off as Jeff entered a highway entrance ramp. Agitated, he'd gassed his Corolla, trailing the truck that merged like a bullet onto the three-lane highway.

The entranceway railing gave way to skyscrapers and blue-sky fizzing outside his windows. Jeff edged his hood at the truck's bumper. The exhaust pipes looked like barrels emerging from a machine-gun turret. The driver was probably rushing home to crank Steel Reserves, polish ARs, he remembered thinking. The truck's brakes flashed. The steering wheel rumbled, and he swerved, then pulled up on the F-150's passenger side. Aswang grew inside him. When the tinted window rolled down, Jeff thought he'd confirm this man was a burly, right-winger. Instead, a cup flew from the truck's cabin, spraying Jeff's windshield in ice and dark soda. He flicked the wipers. Kept on the gas. Ahead, the middle lane slowed, avoiding the highway fork. Jeff was blocked. In the fast lane, the truck roared off. Something caustic and invigorating swam in his vision, and he punched his dashboard.

Back in the kitchen, Jeff added the cracked stereo display to the list of things he needed to fix. Heading into his home office, saturated in unopened letters and tax documents, he flagged Facebook videos, waiting to Zoom with his lawyer. Carolyn knocked.

"It's open."

"Hey, we need to talk." She was a little sweaty, holding a toolbox. Carolyn looked like Ann-Margaret—everything Jeff's parents had admired even before emigrating from the Philippines. Their worship of Elvis followed them to the States and into Jeff's childhood home. A framed photograph of 'the king' was nailed to the wall as if he were family or Panginoong. In a way, Elvis was their god, too. "I put up that flag," she said.

He knew the one she meant. The entire subdivision had one. Jeff imagined their walkway like all the neighbors: haunted by a blue stripe between white and black lines, stiffened in the heat. He'd have to scramble out in the afternoon showers—take the damn thing down. "Guess you're not asking if I minded," he said, smoothing the bandage over his right knuckle. "We don't even believe in *that*."

"It's not the politics. That busybody lady who heads the neighborhood watch asked me about it *again*, so I hung it up. You know, in good faith. It'll be safer. Neighbors will be less edgy. Think of Anthony."

"I do every day."

"I'm sorry—" For a moment, Jeff thought she might use her old pet-name for him. *Honey.* But she didn't. "It's just a flag. It doesn't mean anything."

"Just means you gave in to the cul-de-sac pressure. The cops took hours to go inside—" And before Jeff cursed, he stopped. *Keep the peace.*

"Don't make this about that," Carolyn said, and by the way she tensed, Jeff could tell she was also restraining herself. "If it really bothers you, we can talk tonight. I'm free after Dr. Schaefer's group."

Thursdays, Carolyn went to grief therapy. Jeff half suspected she'd had an affair with her therapist. Last time he'd been dragged to counseling, he lost his temper. They'd gathered in a church community room that doubled as a Montessori during school hours. Carolyn sat next to him in a circle of folded chairs. There were maybe six others.

"Close your eyes," Dr. Schaefer had said. "If you're comfortable."

Jeff was not, but he bowed his head the way he'd done in Mass as a child. He believed Dr. Schaefer preyed on pain, licked his fingers after he dipped into Carolyn's purse for co-pays. Even more so, Jeff loathed the therapist's handsome power, the way everyone in the circle softened when he spoke, nodded emphatically, their eyes moistening. He spoke to Carolyn like an old friend who could heal her in ways Jeff could not.

"Make an object of your grief," Dr. Schaefer said. "In self-compassion, we first recognize the source."

Nope. Not doing that, Jeff thought. Instead, he looked at Schaefer's studded loafers. *Expensive.* That gave Jeff all the right to discredit his integrity.

"Widen that image," the counselor said. "Picture the millions of others hurting in the same way. You are not alone. This is common humanity."

"What a crock of shit," Jeff said under his breath, and when Schaefer ignored him, he said it louder. What had *this man* lost? Jeff thought. "Quack." He said it audibly.

"Mr. Dizon." Dr. Schaefer had aggravating patience. "We'll have time to share at the end of our session."

Jeff felt Carolyn's awareness sear over him. A few of the others in the circle opened their eyes. Were they egging him on, or telling him to shut up? Jeff left, waiting out the session in the car. On the drive home, the radio was loud enough for Lakshmi Singh's reporting to keep the peace.

In the office, Carolyn set the toolbox on his desk. "Maybe this weekend you can take down the swing set?"

He watched Carolyn's neck muscle rise. "Yeah, maybe. If there's time."

"It's been three years."

"I know how long it's been." He imagined frustration could smear like ketchup over a napkin. Be folded into a neat square.

"Have you thought about grad bash?" she asked. "Can Anthony sleep there?"

This was Carolyn's real battle, he thought. The flag tilted the balance her way after he'd forbidden Anthony from spending the night at a Universal Studios trip with his classmates.

"Yeah," Jeff said, his attention back on the laptop. "I still don't think it's a good idea."

"He's a senior," Carolyn said. "Don't rob him of his last chance to have fun with his friends."

ON JEFF'S SCREEN, Luisa sat behind her desk. He noted her charcoal, tailored blazer. Her pencil skirt. When he'd first hired her, in a law office that smelled of cleaning solution and coffee, he'd instantly admired Luisa. She was calm and direct. Never shared the details Jeff refused to watch. Sometimes he fantasized about what a life with her might look like. He'd shudder, force himself to remember Carolyn, even when that reminder felt cold and far off.

"This will be a landmark case," Luisa said. "BWJD agreed to provide a usage license."

"How decent of them." Jeff hated BWJD, the broadcasting company that owned the video; he wanted to sue them bloody. "How's a usage license going to get socials to take down the videos?"

Luisa leaned into her camera. "Do you know what an NFT is?"

Jeff nodded. His firm's management position taught him enough tech minutiae to warn Anthony against playing with crypto. "Copyright infringement?" he asked. "As in, I'll own the footage."

Luisa nodded. "You'll own one of two purported pieces of media. The usage license BWJD's offering won't get Facebook to take down the videos, but if you mint an NFT, yes, you'll own and control the footage that circulates online."

"Then I can sue because it's my property?"

"Owning the video as an NFT gives us basis for litigation, yes." Luisa set her pen in a coffee mug that read "Opposing Counsel Tears" in the bottom right-hand corner of Jeff's screen. "We can seek damages from social media companies still allowing the uploading and sharing of the video."

For the last three years, Jeff had waited for his chance to block conspiracy theorists claiming what had happened to Katie was a hoax. He grimaced, thinking of the comment sections. "Where do I sign?"

"Before paperwork," she said. "Understand, this battle will take years in court. You can change the outcome for a lot of families, but I know you have a son leaving for college, and your wife declined litigation against the school *and* Springfield Armory. It's important your family is prepared for this fight."

Jeff nodded. "We'll do what it takes."

A YEAR BEFORE IT HAPPENED, when Katie was in the second grade, Jeff had picked her up at Vista Point Elementary. His daughter announced she needed to find a junonia shell. Her teacher had assigned a reading on Florida shells, Katie explained. Her classmates were bringing in the seashells they'd found, and Katie *had* to find the rarest. Before, when Jeff and Carolyn had taken her to the beach, shells were boring. Their daughter preferred to punch and kick the incoming surf, pretending they were tidal waves. "Like a power ranger," she'd told them.

"The pink ranger?" Carolyn asked. "That's your favorite, right?"

"No, mommy." Katie flashed her an incredulous look, the look only a seven-year-old, who has the universe solved and neatly aligned, can give; her head tilted, her brown eyes wide. "The yellow ranger!"

Without saying so, Jeff had felt proud. He had cherished their time on the couch bingeing the original episodes, and his daughter identified with Trini Kwan over Kimberly Hart—embraced the one that looked like her. Both kids had taken after him. Beautiful. Filipino eyes. Moles the color of wilted hibiscus. Anthony's below his right eye, Katie's on her forehead.

The seashell mission brought the Dizons to Sanibel Island, shaded under a beach umbrella on towels, except for Katie who combed the shore. Anthony had a get-rich-quick scheme. "Megalodon teeth sell for five thousand bucks."

"Five thousand, huh?" Jeff said. "You'll need six to pay for your first semester of college. You better get out there, son. Katie's gonna beat you to it."

Jeff looked at Katie, thirty feet from where they sat; he'd never seen her so focused. Usually, he'd have to tell her to take a few steps back from the television mounted to their living room wall. Katie's favorite position was standing in a near split, an unwatched iPad in hand, staring point-blank at *Beat Bugs*. Now, at the gulf's edge, she waded through little piles of sea foam, scrutinizing the shoreline. He heard her squeal, and got up to see, but she dropped whatever she'd found, shuffling her feet in semi-circles—one of her classic, frustrated movements.

"Not quite the one?" Jeff asked at her side. He looked down at his determined little girl and saw what she might look like grown: strong-willed tenacity in her shoulders, something like him, but with so much of Carolyn.

"Nope," she said. "But I'll find one."

"Keep looking, girly. You will."

Jeff joined his daughter and was silent. In the silence, Jeff knew she was appreciative—that maybe words were useless in times like this when the best action a father can take is to move his focus alongside his daughter's. Katie broke the silence.

"That's an olive shell. Same shape as the junonia but not the same pattern."

"What about this one?" Jeff bent to pick up what he thought Katie's class of second graders *had* to admire.

Her finger sketched the brown, concentric stripes. "What animal looks like this?"

"A zebra?" Jeff offered.

Katie looked impressed. "That's what Mrs. Beganni told us. It's an arca zebra, but people call them turkey wings."

"Wow!" Jeff indulged her. "Look how smart you are. Doesn't look like a turkey wing to me, though."

"Me either," Katie said, and with what seemed like no thought, hurled the shell into the ocean. "Let's keep looking."

The sand was a brown mosaic. Jeff searched, thinking that if Katie never found this rare shell, he could salvage the day by buying her a sand sifter, a tool. When he turned, Anthony and Carolyn couldn't be seen, but he made out their umbrella, a small dot on the coast. Ahead was the fishing pier. Jeff watched the tide crash against the barnacled pylons.

"Let's walk around," he said. "The pier's dangerous."

HOURS AFTER THE ZOOM with his lawyer, Jeff ran to the grocery store, returning with Vietnamese short ribs. Dizon meals presided over screens.

Dinners were left on the counter, and everyone served themselves, then retreated to their respective lair. Anthony played video games; Carolyn poured over her work's consultant notes; Jeff scoured the Internet, flagging videos. He texted Anthony, who would get a lift home from his coach after soccer practice.

"Home by six. Need help with grill."

When he pulled into the driveway, Carolyn's blue Subaru was parked there. No doubt she'd be upstairs in the bathroom mirror, lathered in her post-work skincare routine. Good, Jeff thought. That'll lighten her mood. He sat in his car, listening to his Corolla's engine clink, remembering their marriage.

On a road trip, before the kids, he and Carolyn had camped in the Everglades.

After a fan boat tour, they'd found their campsite raided by turkey vultures. Carolyn sprinted toward the birds, fearless of their talons. That's how she'll protect our family, he remembered thinking. She was brave. Not like a horror movie—the abandoning of reason—but in a curious way. The type of fearlessness that can discover. In the Sonoran Desert, a purple lightning storm lit up the horizon, pulsing the clouds as if the sky was shattered cathedral glass. Jeff wanted to take cover in the car. Carolyn convinced him of something better. She pointed out a small monolith, the shape of a bulbous thumb, and led them up the thumb where they watched the storm—all that natural energy discarding itself in a fury the color of ube over the saguaro cacti. Lightning hitchhiked Carolyn's face, flashing away the shadows. Jeff had thought her excitement was pure. That no matter how hard the skies trembled, with her, life could be curious. A discovery.

In their bedroom, he asked about her day to the open bathroom door. His dress shoes hung off the palm-patterned duvet. On the bedside tables were photographs. Wide, candid smiles. One in front of Disney's Cinderella Castle, another in North Carolina at Sliding Rock. These, no one took down. From the bathroom, terse silence.

He knew she'd heard him. "How was your day?"

A pause long enough for him to pull out his phone, open a few apps.

"Fine," Carolyn said finally. "Thanks for asking. How was yours?"

He darkened the phone screen. Anthony hadn't texted him back.

"I met with Luisa," he said, feeling a resentful pulse from Carolyn when he said his lawyer's name. "I have good news."

She walked out, still wearing dress pants, but had taken off her shirt; one of her conservative bras lifted her breasts, wrists against her sides. "Again, with this?" she said. "You know I want the same thing you do."

"This is different."

He barely detected her sigh. "Fine. Tell me."

"Luisa said if we mint an NFT, we can sue Facebook. It'll be like owning a car title, but the car's the video. We can make them take it down."

"That won't stop people. They'll find a way. Always do."

"This time—"

"Jeff, *honey*. So what? Delete your Facebook. Get a hobby. Don't you miss playing ball with Nathaniel and Luis?"

Jeff hadn't gone for a Y pickup game in years. "This is important," he said. "We can stop psychopaths from using a video of our—" Jeff disciplined his octaves. "We can control this now." The photos smiled at him from the bedside table. "We can destroy it."

Carolyn sat on the bed's corner, looking at him the way she had when he first hired Luisa—the look before the arguments when Jeff relinquished control and deferred: no prosecution. "It's not a good idea." Her face disappeared in her phone.

An old quote, one he couldn't place, fired in Jeff's mind.

When good do nothing...

"No one will be able to watch it," he said. "It'll keep her name out of their conspiracies." Carolyn's face turned steel, and Jeff pleaded. "Please, if we own the video, this won't happen again. You have to be on the same page with me."

Evil triumphs.

"It's not a good idea." She stood from the bed. "We need to focus on healing, not chasing down online conspiracists."

"What about the flag?" Jeff also stood. "You hung that up without even asking me."

"You know it's smarter that way." Carolyn hugged herself, covering her chest. "I would like to start planting my garden soon, before summer, and it's too hot. Can you take down the swings, please? Tomorrow?"

"Yeah, I'll try," Jeff said without thinking.

"Please get dinner started. Anthony texted. He'll be home soon."

JEFF OPENED the sliding glass door to his backyard, where Anthony was cutting the ribs into small chunks on the grill's side table. His son didn't look like he needed help.

"You're cutting them?" Jeff asked.

"Traditionally," Anthony said. "That's how suon ram man is prepared." Cooking had always fascinated Anthony. Even when he was younger, he loved culinary tutorials. Last time Jeff really knew him, Anthony claimed his TikTok chef channel would go viral. He'd be rich. Somewhere along the way that spark had died. Probably from Jeff's rants.

"Guess you know what you're doing," Jeff said. Further out in the yard, he glanced at the swing set, covered in a swarm of crane flies hovering over the rubber seats. He looked away.

"Can I help?"

"I need tin foil."

"Don't we want grill marks?"

Anthony shook his head. "Nope. Really, we should be sauteing these."

Jeff eyed the instructions. "You sure?"

"Positive."

"Recipe on the back says grill evenly on both sides."

"That's Trader Joe's," Anthony said. "I'll make them how they're supposed to be made."

Jeff returned from the kitchen with tin foil and watched his son. The grill temperature rose. Sweat rolled down his sides.

"Have you thought about grad bash?" Anthony placed the ribs in the center grate. "You gonna let me sleep at the hotel?"

Here it is, Jeff thought, the inevitable. He'd raked this question over his mind until his brain needed sutures. Anthony wanted something so simple: stay up at night joking, play pranks, maybe even sneak off for some teenage romance—normal things that Jeff had done in his childhood. But an image had burrowed into his brain, the hemisphere that controlled fear. Everywhere. Men with guns left holes where none should be. Yeah, Universal had security, but the hotel wouldn't. Neither would the highway. Maybe this was irrational like the NFT, Jeff thought, but he couldn't lose another one.

"Yeah, son. I still don't think it's a good idea. Going is one thing, but staying the night. You know why I can't let you, right?"

Anthony sucked his teeth and opened the grill. "Yeah, I guess." Smoke, muddled with vinegar and pineapple, wafted their faces. "Mom said it'd be fine. Literally every senior is going."

"I'd let you if I could." He wanted to touch his son's shoulder but wouldn't be able to stand Anthony flinching away. "I need to do everything I can to keep you safe. You get that, right?"

"I get it, Dad. You're scared something will happen."

"I trust *you*, son. It's the world—."

"It's fine," Anthony sighed. "We all knew you'd never let me."

This broke Jeff to the blood cell. Couldn't Anthony throw the ribs on the ground? Scream the way Jeff cursed reckless drivers? He'd conceded so easily. Anthony saw right through him, to the scared dad who didn't even know how to grill suon ran man.

THAT NIGHT, Jeff couldn't sleep. He stood over the kitchen sink. The window was dark, but he knew what was in his own backyard. Out the front door, he passed the dark flag on his way for a drive. He'd crank old tunes. Question whichever god might listen. Maybe he'd get fast food? Inhale greasy fries so salty, when he chewed, they'd taste like drugs.

Past the suburbs, he drove down a busy three-lane road. His LED screen flickered from the crack he'd made, but he could still listen to an old Tool song. Back in college, Jeff thought the song's misanthropy was poetic without considering the irony that this '90s music filled with anger were party tunes back then. He nodded to lyrics, praying for Armageddon's tidal waves to come sooner, and an old thought emerged. His parents had always grumbled that life had gotten worse, society decayed, even in the States. Wasn't that what every generation said to their children? That the world was worse. He knew the answer now.

Pray for tidal waves.

Jeff stopped at a red light, ready to turn left into a Jollibee. Across the pedestrian walkway on his left, he noticed someone crossing. Looked like a woman, but he couldn't be sure. Was she holding something against her chest? A little late to be walking around with an infant, he thought. Behind him, a Nissan's rumbling exhaust system pulled up. In his rearview, he squinted against the headlights. The turning arrow flashed green. The car behind him honked. *Someone's crossing the street, asshole. Hold on.* The car honked again, then pulled around Jeff's Toyota, headlights disfiguring the night, and shot through the green. In the intersection, the Nissan's brakes screeched, nearly colliding with the crossing woman. The Nissan swerved around her, and when she made her way past the median, Jeff followed. Nearly killed that woman, he fumed. He'd get his plates, scold him. He swerved to the driver's side and pointed: *roll down your window.* When he did, Jeff saw a heavyset man.

"You could've killed that woman," he yelled.

"She shouldn't have been crossing a green," the man yelled back.

Ahead, the light was turning yellow. The Nissan lurched forward, beating the light that turned red as Jeff tailed him.

At the next red, the heavy man got out. And lifted his shirt. "Stop following me." Tucked in his waistband was a pistol.

Jeff didn't know if this asshole had the gall. Probably the type that bought a gun for a moment like this—brandish a piece without ever throwing a punch. Jeff stepped out of his car. He was too angry to know if he needed this man to be the one who had filmed the video or be his tidal wave.

"Learn how to fucking drive," he said. "You could've killed that woman and her baby."

"Dude, she was holding a liquor bottle. Back up, or I stand my ground."

Jeff swung. Hard as he could. A sharp pain ran up his forearm, and his eyes watered. He tried hiding the pain.

The man massaged his cheek. "You hit like a bitch," he scoffed. "Go home before you get yourself killed."

He got back in his Nissan and sped off, leaving Jeff alone in the empty street, his hand throbbing. What am I even trying to save anymore? he thought. The dangerous man with the gun got away, and for the second time that week, he'd thrown a punch and only hurt himself.

WHEN HE GOT HOME, he went to his son's door. Anthony's room was dark except for a yellow sliver of hallway light seeping from the hallway.

He listened to his son's breath, soft and contented, there. Nervous his son might wake, and he'd have to explain why he was standing over him watching Anthony's chest rise and fall, Jeff left down the hallway.

In the home office, he sat down, flipped open his laptop, and pushed the toolbox Carolyn had left there against the wall. BWJD had used the word *grisly*. The video was nine minutes and eighteen seconds. Went viral the day it happened. He'd never watched the footage and wouldn't start tonight. He found Luisa's email. The process was simple: first, he created the accounts, the crypto wallet and digital marketplace account; second, he uploaded the video and selected a preview, the footage's first image, a blurred flash of Vista Point's hallway, then he named the NFT. *Junonia*. He hit create and waited.

The video processed.

YEARS AGO, on the beach search for Katie's shell, Jeff and his daughter walked the shore. The Gulf waters lapped their heels. Foamy waves unfolded the sand, exposing the rolling shells, burrowing back into the shoreline before the next wave excavated them in an endless cycle. Fifteen feet ahead stood the pier. Katie was determined to search there, through the barnacled pylons bristling against a churning ocean.

"We either go around the pier or we head back, kiddo."

She argued. "What if that's the only place on this whole beach with a junonia." She pointed, and Jeff imagined barbed hooks in the sand from cut fishing lines snagged on the seabed. Katie continued. "People look everywhere but under the pier."

Jeff squished his mouth. For a seven-year-old, she made a good point. He glanced behind him, though he knew Carolyn couldn't see them. If their daughter got even the tiniest scratch, they'd both be grounded. "Katie, you're not listening. It's dangerous. If we're not listening, that tells me it's time to go back."

"Please, Daddy. You can hold my hand the whole time like we're crossing the street."

She might as well have been a million water-eyed puppies. Jeff took her hand, urged her to stay close, and they waded under the pier. He braced her little body against the waves, kept Katie on her feet—safe from anything sharp. Together, they searched. But the wooden slats above shined only pockets of light in the murky, agitated water. The sun moved through the sky, the tide pulled, and Jeff's back began to ache. "Katie," he said, sensing she already knew. "It's time."

She crouched, yanking up sand. She'd learned to bury her frustrations in movement: a cartwheel when she couldn't figure out math homework, wringing her favorite blanket, the one with the Power Rangers, into a corkscrew before her infamous bedtime. Mud sifted through her fingers. No junonia.

"We'll find one," Jeff said. An unrequited smile. "We'll get a shell sifter. That'll make this easier."

They headed back, and for his daughter's sake, Jeff trawled his pupils over the beach for the brown-spotted, spindle-shaped treasure. He thought about the shell's name. Junonia, for Juno, Jupiter's wife. The fearless protector goddess who ruled over the home like Carolyn. Would she have let Katie under the pier? Maybe. At least now he shared this secret with his daughter—he'd allowed some mild danger and kept her free of scratches, safe. But all in vain without the shell.

Ahead, underneath the umbrella, were two figures, and as they drew closer, the figures' details grew into his wife and son. Katie was brooding further behind as they entered the Dizon's beach camp. Soon, everyone had enough sun, and boardwalk ice cream peppered their conversation. Jeff agreed. They'd head out.

Before leaving, he walked back to the shoreline. One last shot. He thought of the elementals his mother had told him about as a boy: Filipino superstitions to respect the Dalaketnons for safe passage. He dug his fingers into the sand—as Katie had done—and felt something cylindrical. He felt silly when his heart leaped. Whatever this was had to be trash, some other boring shell, as his daughter would've described, but what he pulled from the mud had brown spots over a creamy spindle. "Katie, look!"

She came down from where she'd been upwind, flapping sand from her towel at Anthony. Her brows were narrow, skeptical. Jeff tossed her the shell. She squealed, pawing the shell as if to make sure the brown spots wouldn't wash away, making sure the junonia was real. Katie wrapped her tiny body around Jeff's leg, squeezing his calf as if she wanted that latch to hold forever, as if he could absorb her little life force, become one person. Jeff walked with Katie's body wrapped around his leg.

"You find a Megalodon tooth?" Anthony asked.

"Better!" Katie said. No signs of releasing Jeff's leg. "Daddy found the junonia!"

That day, Jeff had felt like a father who could control the fates and tides. He'd protected her from the barnacles. Even made a little magic appear in the sand. Worthy of his wife and children.

THE SCREEN LOADED.

The video was full resolution, not the thumbnail from the previous page. Jeff saw the perspective of a rifle designed for the Vietnam War, a camera mounted to the barrel. The rifle panned a hallway, sweeping from one set of lockers to where classroom doors were closed.

He shut his laptop.

THE BED SHEETS were taut over Carolyn's body. Jeff fumbled his way next to her in the dark. She stirred, and he thought she might pull away, but she rolled closer, resting her arm on his leg. He slid against her clavicle, breathing in her scent like hang-dried linen.

"Where were you?"

"I went out," he said. "Had to think."

"You're still processing. Dr. Schaefer says that's natural."

True. When it first happened, Jeff bottled. Then, almost at random, at red lights or a break in the evening news, he wept a deep, uncontrollable well buried in his gut, as if bereavement could only surface if wrangled from the deep of his organs where tears were folded away like napkins.

"What did you think about?" Carolyn asked.

"Anthony."

Carolyn hugged her pillow, facing the wall. "He told me you're still not letting him sleep at grad bash."

Jeff sighed. "He hates me."

"Even if that's true," Carolyn said. "You should let him go. Not to win him over. Let him go because it's what's right."

The fan whirred.

"I made the NFT," Jeff said.

Carolyn sucked her teeth. "And how did that make you feel?"

"It still hurts."

"It always will."

"Fuck," Jeff said, because he had nothing better to offer.

Carolyn rolled over, and he could see her blond wisps in the moonlight. "Tomorrow, I'm telling Anthony he can sleep in Orlando. Or you can tell him yourself."

The moon cut through the blinds.

"Okay," said Jeff, picturing himself going against his word. "I'll tell him he can go." Soon as he said the words, he knew he meant them.

Carolyn yawned then brushed his thigh. "About time."

"Listen, if I use my bonus, take nothing from Anthony's college fund, I can go after the people posting the video." Carolyn sat up. "Before you say anything," Jeff continued. "Know I'm doing this so we don't have to see it anymore. This can help the other families. They live with this, too. I own this now. They can't use what I own. We just have to fight. Will you fight with me?"

"Let's take it one day at a time," said Carolyn.

"Okay," Jeff said again. "One more thing."

"Oh God, what?"

"Let's take down that flag."

Jeff couldn't believe Carolyn was laughing. "Only if you tell the neighborhood watch lady."

Jeff's turn to laugh. "You scared of Karen?"

"I'm not scared of her, idiot. She's annoying. I want to punch her in the face."

"I know the feeling," said Jeff. "I'll talk to her."

Carolyn yawned. "Give her hell, honey," she said, pulling the sheets higher.

Jeff closed his eyes. In the first years of marriage, Carolyn was on the edge of his every thought and decision. The way she'd pressed her forehead against his mother's when they danced at their wedding, his mother in a bayabas-green dress against her bride's white. Then marveling at her through Anthony, then Katie's births. He thought of their love as an animal. Love grew, had a capacity. From fierce and binding, to now, simply the comfort of having shared almost everything with this person.

Even loss.

In the morning, Jeff went to the kitchen, brewed coffee, and looked out the window. When his mug was drained, he crossed the room to the sliding glass door and walked into the backyard, toolbox in hand, toward the swing set where he used to push Katie as high as her fearlessness would let him. ◆

BRIANNA STEIDLE

RED RIGHT RETURN

Headlights leap along the guardrail
like prey-animals. You're old enough to see
nothing's darting from the treeline.
Nothing's disappearing
around the bend. All along the coast
condos bow toward the ocean. Does she know
that video of the octopus changing colors
as it dreams? You'd love
to ask, but where she is, the sun is
already rising. Tomorrow you'll wake
to all your trees shrinkwrapped
with fog. You'll be the same color
you were last night, and the dreams will have leaked
down the sink.   So there you are, not ocean bound,
driving down the Florida Turnpike, smelling smoke
against a blind sky, trusting somewhere out of sight
sugarcane fields are burning.

LISA ZERKLE

LONG DISTANCE

It's early my father calls he says I can't remember exactly what he says some-thing like if you have anything to say to her say it now I'm staying in a chain hotel somewhere in the middle of Tokyo my room like all the others a dresser two beds split by a night stand holding up the light my children deep in their teenage sleep I say what do I say I can't remember my exact words here it's morning there night did he say it's your last chance I take the phone to the bathroom she has a bed in a for-profit hospital in north Atlanta I hear her breathing the hiss and pump of oxygen I say something like it's okay you can go here it's tomorrow there today she's dying today the longest day of the year she's breathing I hear her she says my name says it as a question my chil-dren sleep tomorrow's today it's late the phone rings where am I my father calls he says I can't remember exactly something like she's gone when they wake we stand together at the window the city spread before us arteries and buildings as far as we can see all these people none we know what to do I tell them I tell them she's gone

HILL RUSHING LUM

JUMPER

My younger brother Ralph was two when we started calling him a jumper. At first it was amusing. The couch, the bed, the step-down in front of the house we leased-to-own from Mister Rennaker. Sometimes it sounded like my parents called him Master Rennaker. The misters I knew had stern jaws and kind eyes. They fed us pieces of their apples with their pocketknives as we ran between houses. They let us sneak pieces of cake if we brought them some. The man who stood at my parents' door with his thumb in his belt loops didn't look like those misters. He had splotchy skin and messy shirts with hot dog ketchup and underarm sweat. He looked exactly like the kind of man who wouldn't fix the concrete stoop that tripped everyone when they came over for religious holidays or funeral parties. He wore his frown like a person who wasn't going to fix the broken things. The kind of man who called the cops when my father and uncle and cousins leaned against the fence and drank canned beer and laughed loudly so the women knew nothing bad had happened. The kind of man who believed darker skin is something that can be beaten white if given enough time, bills, parole. Even though it's the same color as the thick thighs on the pretty girls he watched down by Stylze Nailz. He looked exactly like the kind of man who would pay a girl like that to mess his shirt.

Each time Ralph jumped he became a little braver. The heights a little higher, the falls a little harder. We plucked bits of grit from his scrapes and scratches and tallied the rocks and gravel. We argued if the bloody fragments counted as *wholes* or *less-thans*. The same way we argued about whether we were going to let Monica pretend to be a princess after she got the pink shoes with a kitten heel from Goodwill. We had seen Monica's sister wear a fancy dress and tiara for a birthday last year, so we knew it was possible to be something more than what everyone always sees. And when we watched her pack up her boyfriend's car with boxes of clothes and dishes and homemade bread recipes, we knew enough of the right things could make a whole thing. It didn't matter that her grandparents' two-bedroom house with its tinfoil window coverings and makeshift carport wasn't a castle—it was barely ever a home. But Monica's secondhand shoes were scuffed and smelled like spray can deodorant, and her hair was always getting tangled in her mouth, and sometimes she wiped her nose on her hand. Those were enough less-thans that no one wanted to pretend she was better than us. And the rocks covered in coagulated blood were counted as less-thans because no one wanted to take them home, except Ralph who counted all the rocks as wholes. And we let him since he was the jumper and because he couldn't count very high.

My aunts counted as high as our loose teeth and the flies that came in through the holes in the screen door. My mother counted on her fingers the number of times everything was my fault. When she got to her pinky she started over. I counted cracks in the ceiling when my father lectured me for not being more watchful. When the homily lengthened with the light coming through the kitchen window, I began counting squares formed by other square tiles. Eventually my grandfather shuffled from the back bedroom and put his swollen hands on my father's shoulder to remind everyone this was only temporary.

-2-

"Oh, Maria, your brother jumped all the time. I thought he was going to break every bone," my grandmother consoled my mother as they shared the mirror to pluck their eyebrows and draw them back in. When the house got too hot and the days too long, they would forget such intimacy and circle each other like crows to pluck out eyes with press-on nails.

In the end, my grandmother would wipe away any tears and messes with her sleeves. If she had longer arms and bigger blouses, she would have wiped us all from this forgotten street. Our lives would be absorbed in the soft cotton, making our way along the welt threads to the warmth of her chest that smelled like butter and powder perfume.

When she died, I cut the sleeves off some of her blouses and hid them under my pillow. At night I held onto them the way other children held stuffed animals or old blankets. I wept for the return of her arms around me or for my mother to like me better or for my father to find a new job or for the boy who sat next to me in math to stop writing hateful words on his desk. Some days after school I found the sleeves had already been used by someone else's grief. If it was my mother, she never let me know. Just like I never let the boy in math class know his words got to me.

-3-

The year Ralph was five, my parents took him to the emergency room three times. The first was after he jumped off the tall kitchen stool. He was given secondhand shoes from our cousin Mike. Ralph complained they were too big, three sizes too big, clown shoes too big. But everyone insisted he would grow into them. And maybe he would have, eventually. But when he landed, he tripped over cousin Mike's three-sizes-too-big clown shoes and hit his forehead against the counter and needed six stitches. The shoes needed a new home, another cousin to wear them until the soles peeled away. But we kept the tall kitchen stool because it was the one my Uncle Mario used when he complained about his back and rubbed his lumbar until the color faded from his shirts.

"Mariposa, get me my chair." Sometimes the words tangled up in his push-broom mustache, and he plucked them out for me. He shook his finger with silent directions. *No, no, over there, yes, yes, that's good.* Then he sat tall, one cowboy boot on the bottom rung, the other dangling free, occasionally being used to slow down a child or scratch a dog's neck.

I'm not sure Uncle Mario really needed the stool for any serious condition, except maybe the one where he needed to be as tall as my father when they were in the same room. Uncle Mario isn't my real uncle. We were all told to call him that because he knew my father longer than my mother did. At some point in time, Uncle Mario and my father were the same. Same wandering brown eyes. Same unruly dark hair. Same height from fingertip to fingertip. But then one day my father woke up, as he tells it, and he wasn't the same. His eyes stopped moving around like they used to. And his hair laid down real nice with a part on the side. And he had grown six, no seven, maybe ten inches taller than Uncle Mario. That was the day he noticed my mother because he could see her over all the heads in the crowd. My mother would scoff, but then my father scooped her in his arms and said sweet things, like the way her skin looked in the morning light or the way her eyes smiled at him from across the room or the way she smelled when he got close enough to say hello and how, when he learned her name, he held it in his mouth like an old fashioned Christmas candy to savor the sweetness until it melted away.

-4-

When Ralph went to the emergency room the second time that year, it was because he jumped off the side of the bathtub. It wasn't a big jump. He wanted to see what it would feel like, creating a Ralph-size hole in the thick foam bubbles. His toes curled over the rim. His feet wet. His excitement great. He jumped to avoid falling, like we all do. He didn't think about the soap dish that stood proud from the wall. It knocked our elbows when we bathed, bumped our heads when we played pirates, hit our backs when we were mermaids, in a tub barely big enough for one. The sound of the Ralph-shaped hole spilling over the edge yelled for my mother. She pulled his body close and screamed for my father.

Forehead wounds bleed readily. The blood vessels run under the skin waiting for an escape, an opening, a split for eruption. Red mixed with the wet and made watercolor rivers down Ralph's cheeks. The liberated tributaries stained my mother's dress while she sat on the floor, in the car, in the waiting room. My father carried him through the double doors like a wounded soldier, a t-shirt smashed against his forehead like a war rag. I didn't understand the way my parents cradled Ralph in guilt. It wasn't their choice to jump or fall. It was barely even Ralph's. He got seven stitches. My parents got a dose of Diazepam.

Everyone talked about it for weeks. My parents blamed me. My grandfather blamed the builder. My father wanted to call Master Rennaker to have the soap dish removed but decided it would probably make things worse. My mother lamented while she folded laundry or washed dishes, loud enough for my father's attention but with her back turned to spare him the shame of being helpless. *Why did they put it there? It's good for nothin. It doesn't even hold the soap.*

But I liked the plop sound when the soap jumped from the curved ceramic into my bath water. My fingers wrestled pieces trying to escape through the drain holes. I squeezed the slimy parts like they were an extension of me. I was the sliver breaking from the world, looking for a way out, slithering through the openings only to be caught by jagged fingernails. My mother's words holding me back. *Quit. Don't. No.* Short words keeping me on a short leash.

I prefer longer words. Each syllable tells the whole story. Short words are less-thans. Nobody wants to take them home and put them on their special shelf. The shelf that holds the pumice stone from the river hike and the old perfume bottle that was only twenty-five cents from an estate sale and a poetry book by Rupi Kaur found at the Little Free Library and an empty matchbox that smells like winter.

Wait is a less-than word. When my teacher said *wait*, I replied *until when?* But *moratorium* is a whole word. When Mr. Tate at the pawn shop said there's a moratorium on hiring men like my father, I knew he was telling a whole story. The story about how people couldn't find work like they used to, and drinking was cheaper than paying the gas bill. That's why his shop was so busy and why I couldn't hang around too much in case one of the men, the ones having to pawn their watches and guitars, got a little rambunctious. *Rambunctious* is also a whole word. It can mean the kids filled with too much sugar who are howling at the sky and barking at the dog and pulling each other's shirts when playing tag. Or it could mean an uncontrollable man wanting to take back his power by having a pocket-sized bottle of Ten High and forcing his strength and virility between youthful legs.

Stop is a less-than word. Because no one ever listens to it.

-5-

The third emergency room visit wasn't too bad. Ralph jumped off the wall separating our yard from the neighbor's dog. But the fall twisted his foot, and his knee looked like someone stuffed rolled-up socks under his skin. After that my parents required regular house checks for a little while. The hospital was suspicious Ralph was being mistreated. *Negligent* was the word they used, the story the doctors wanted to tell. But my parents weren't inattentive, not like the city when it didn't remove the soiled and bloodied mattress someone dumped in the empty lot near our house. The one my father and Uncle Mario threw in the back of the truck and hauled away because they were worried we were seeing our future. My parents weren't irresponsible, not like the dispensary a few streets over that sells vape pens to middle school kids for extra cash. My parents weren't careless like the police officer who shot that boy from my history class, the one riding in the front seat of the car when his dad was pulled over. The news showed the body cam of an angry man. But I saw a dad tired of being asked to get out of the car while his son was holding a drive-thru kid's meal. My parents weren't negligent. They didn't kill Ralph.

The social worker came by four times, each scheduled in advance. Ralph and I sat at the kitchen table playing cards while she asked my parents a list of questions. I answered them in my head and collected threes and jacks.

Who lives in your house?

All of us. When Mrs. Paula's husband is in a bad mood, she stays the night on the couch. Monica stays in my bed when she's afraid to walk home, and my mother gives her my eggs in the morning. My grandmother lived here before the cancer spread. I think the cancer is still on the sheets my grandfather sleeps on.

How long are your children left alone?

Always. When the house is shrinking, Ralph and I are shoved out of rooms to walk the streets like dogs and return for supper when the streetlights turn on. My parents are alone even when they sit next to each other. All the houses are filled with loneliness, which is why they are all filled with the junk no one wants.

Do you argue in front of your children?

It's when they don't, when we hear their heated whispers from behind the curtained door, that we sit with our arms around our knees and guess who is sick or if our parents will get a divorce or, worse, if we'll have to move again.

Do you hit your child?

My mother only hits me in anger, otherwise she wouldn't hit me. Ralph is never hit. My father says girls shouldn't be hit past a certain age. It's the same age boys come into the world and should be hit repeatedly.

How long have you been unemployed?

I glanced at my father to hear his answer, but Ralph was yelling he won. All his cards were red.

-6-

"Oh, Maria, boys need more room to grow than girls," my aunt reassured my mother as they dyed each other's hair the same dark shade of darker. A few days later they forgot this act of sisterhood and complained to their husbands about missing shower caps and unanswered texts. They picked at old scars and squeezed the blood out until it dripped down their skin the way the dye dripped into the sink.

Ralph didn't need space. He needed to jump. He jumped off the hood of Uncle Mario's new used-car. He jumped four branches up from a park tree. He jumped off the folded-up gym bleachers with all the little brown eyes watching him like he was their television superhero.

Nothing my parents did stopped him. Eventually they gave up, the way we all do at some point. Instead, they reminded everyone how to accept the inevitable with notes taped to his backpack or stapled to his jacket or pinned to his sweaters. *I think Ralph is going to jump off the roof today. Ralph's wrist is swollen, but it's not the hand he uses to learn. Ralph's head is hurting, watch for signs of a concussion.*

My parents didn't fasten reminders to me. In eighth grade my father forgot to pick me up from the library. I waited outside curled around my backpack. My shoes grew roots in the crack. A spider built a web between my bent head and the rows of brick that separated fiction from reality. I was hoping my parents had gotten into a terrible car accident or the house had caught on fire. Some disastrous or unescapable event was preventing them from reaching me. When the librarian told me she had talked to my parents, I knew the only tragedy was my own.

"Why are you this way?" my mother asked when she picked me up hours later. The windows were down because the AC was broken. I watched her pull the passenger door handle that only worked from the inside. My grandfather said things broke when the season changed. But it felt like the seasons never changed here because nothing ever got fixed.

As we drove, I told my mother about what happened at the park earlier in the week, and the way a man at the grocery store looked at me, and the sick feeling I got in my stomach sometimes late at night that hurt so bad I threw up. She just shook her head, in disbelief or knowing, I didn't know which.

My mother was good at disguising her meanings, like the way she said my aunt's cooking was the best, but never got seconds. Or when she bullied my father to stay at home instead of going to Leo's for two, four, or seven beers, then treated him like he chose to go anyway. The way she softly kissed my head goodnight but then pretended she didn't hear me when I asked for more.

At the liquor store she got out of the van to buy two lottery tickets. One was never enough. Three and people thought we were running from our problems. I muttered the word *insignificant* under my breath, worried she might hear me and march back through the store door with its beer posters and gun warnings to snatch my cheeks and dare me to repeat myself. Like the time I said I wasn't her slave after she told me to do the dishes. She pressed my lips together so hard I thought she was going to suck out my spite the way our priest says the devil will take our souls. Other times it feels like she's squishing my cheeks with her mind as she stares into my eyes and mouths *go*. One of the few short words that tells everything.

I spent the next few days taping and gluing and sticking bits of paper all over the house that said *Do not forget me*. Except *me* is a less-than word.

-7-

My name has enough syllables to be a whole word. But my mother would smash the sounds together so tightly there wasn't room for my name to stretch. I would yell for her to stop, but she didn't because it's too small a word. Then my mother would say my name louder, smaller. And the more my name felt cramped and suffocated, the more I wanted it to be set free from her mouth. I would throw myself on the floor gasping for her deliverance, but she only thought I was throwing a tantrum the way Christina's little sister did when she didn't get to watch television. It ended when my mother used the word *disappointment*, which is a very long word, and left the room.

The year I went to summer school because of my absences, my parents didn't notice I was gone all day. The teacher didn't remember me. She mispronounced my name in June and July the same way she had in August through May. It was the same summer I got grounded for hurting my mother's back. My little cousins told her I had been jumping on cracks all afternoon. I told her I had balanced on the sidewalk fissures, the places too stressed to hold themselves together, waiting for a circus troupe or ballet company or world gymnastic coaches to see me walk wonders from a great distance and scoop me up away from this place. This crack-infested neighborhood with its window-mounted ACs that only blew warm air, and the cars piled along the curbs so the garbage trucks couldn't take our trash and the way people stared like we didn't belong here when we were from here. My mother was hurt more by my truth than her superstition.

She grounded me indefinitely. *Indefinitely* is a long word often used incorrectly.

When the middle school threatened to expel Ralph after he jumped off the gymnasium, my parents sent handwritten apology notes tied to cookie tins. They didn't forget anyone. They remembered the principal and teachers and educational aids and coaches and custodians. But they forgot my birthday the next week because they were busy fighting about whether they could afford the drive to the alternative school. My parents were spending their time and money worrying about finding a job that didn't ask too many questions, and bills they paid in cash and the color of the water and their children's sins.

The school didn't worry, not when they realized my parents forgot to ask the important questions. *How did he get up there? Why didn't you call us sooner? What do you mean this happened before?*

But I asked those questions to Ralph when we were lying on his bed watching muted TV. My parents muffled sounds dubbed over the late afternoon soap opera my grandmother used to watch. I could hear my mother angry-crying, which made me uncomfortable because I never knew if she was angry at me or sad for me. Through hot tears she would whisper my name, and it would stick on her chapped lips until she spat it out with her tongue, leaving a lipstick stain on my name when she was done.

He looked at me the way I looked at my parents when they asked me stupid questions. *How was your day? Where have you been?*

We were surrounded by expectations and limits, people doing the same thing but waiting for something different to happen. A lottery ticket left on the fridge past its date. An expired pawn ticket left in my father's pants. My mother's prayers over the stretched rosary. We tried to stay inside the lines. But so do drunks and immigrants, which made it harder for someone to tell us or them apart. We knew the path wasn't found somewhere between the left side and the right side of the street. No silent directions in life to follow. *No, no, over there, yes, yes, that's good*. All we had were my polysyllabic recitals and Ralph's jumps.

We watched the soundless scenes until my father entered with a heavy sigh.

"Why must you keep doing this?" He sounded like my mother; I wonder if he felt ashamed for using her words instead of his.

Ralph turned his eyes from the glowing picture box, but he didn't sit up. "Because I have to do something." He didn't say anything else. He turned his eyes back to the television, but he wasn't watching it anymore. I waited for my father to respond, but he didn't. He was no longer the man that could carry fifty men on his back or stop a moving train or fly my mother to the moon on his dreams or say I love you. He got up and left us in the dark.

"It'll happen. One day I'll have a jump that will change things."

"You mean *transformation*." And we both pretended to watch the silenced actors.

-9-

"Oh, Maria, if your son keeps acting like this, he'll never grow up," chided a neighbor over tea. My mother said I was too old to run around outside and tangle my hair, throw sticks, or myself, at the boys down the street. Her hand rested on my knee, and she squeezed my leg when I opened my mouth. She threw her voice asking for more sugar to swallow the pungent drink and bitter words.

Ralph and I used to walk across the overpass when my parents needed something, and the van didn't work or they were too tired to get out of bed. We used to pretend the bridge was a magical road that took us from waiting to having, from suffering to whatever was on the other side of suffering. When we stopped at the top, somewhere in the middle of behind and forward, we watched the cars drive underneath us as the wind slammed our bodies against the guardrail. We took turns guessing where everyone was going. *The mall. The mountains. Disneyland.*

Sometimes the overpass was shut down because of a fatality. The officials usually blamed it on a drunk driver. They never blamed it on the bartender who poured too many drinks or the friend who didn't take the keys. They never blamed it on Victoria who broke up with my cousin the day he got fired and texted him he was worthless, and she wanted a real man. We stopped blaming Victoria when we saw her at the funeral, puffy-eyed and red-nosed, and when we saw our aunt hold her like she was her own. My aunt only blamed herself for thinking those words. Truth and superstition are sometimes the same thing.

The day after Ralph turned sixteen, he and I walked the overpass to the liquor store to find our father's missing wallet. By then the bridge was only ever concrete, stretched from one side of waiting to the other side of waiting. A place for fast cars driven by people who only saw us long enough to avoid us. The middle was just an equal point in a greater distance.

Long words are better than short ones. *Discovery. Self-actualization. Freedom.*

But not all short words are less-thans. *Pain. Wish. Ralph.*

The underpass was shut down for a few hours, and the officials didn't blame anyone. My parents didn't blame me. At the funeral my mother held me like I had always been her own. She spoke my name slowly, letting each syllable fall from her mouth. My parents used Ralph's name like a balloon, sounding it out like it had four, five, or nine phonemes, each distinct sound lifting their fears and dreams and love and hurt above them.

I stood in the doorway of our lease-to-own house with its crooked stoop and outdated bath dish and watched my parents pack the van, say goodbye to neighbors, accept Pyrex dishes covered in foil. I saw my mother quiet-cry with every hug and give extra kisses when asked. I saw my father touch the small of her back that had missed him over the years. I watched them reach for Ralph, changing the memories to hold his hand a little tighter, a little longer. I understood my parents' repentance, the way I understood my salvation.

As we left, kids played tag in the street and around the cars, dogs barked behind rusted iron gates. Farther down, a boy stood on top of a tall, brick wall, looking for something far away, waiting for something that was supposed to happen. There's only one thing to do that high up. The girls below him squealed and yelled *jump.* ◆

JEFF MCRAE

A KIND OF PROMISE

For Mr. Ulrich

Rain falls on the gymnasium roof
so we turn on a dime and sit five minutes
listening with the lights off. *Shh.*
Hunger seeps through the second grade.
Thunder rumbles in the unseen sky.
Her daddy packed a box of raisins
for lunch. *I really like your short hair!*
I can see eggs. They've lived there
since last year, her nape bloody with bites.
Across the ceiling and down the walls,
pipes channel the water around our
make-do rows. I slip a set of watercolors
I bought the night before into her desk
and say, *Paint me a picture of your*
favorite animal. Two days later, she
brings a dream, a unicorn. Her family
was kicked out of Tennessee.
The whole thing, she says. It's now
a mythic place she remembers as
the sound of cars outside a motel.
The pandemic landed us in the gym,
far from the old room and other groups,
where last year a string section
played Mendelssohn and years ago
my son hit the winning shot
on a dead-ball foul. Now we're rows
and columns beneath the cranked-back
backboard, the hoop netted with
a papier-mache butterfly, hung
like some changed and beautiful

fragile thing. Metamorphosis
is a kind of promise. I cut her an apple
and smear on peanut butter. We're
learning to make change, to read,
to write haiku, to predict how many
almonds fit inside a jar.

LAURA ROSENTHAL

GRETEL SPEAKS

It's the happy ending that kills me.
Look, I heard my own parents plot my death.
I pretended to believe them when they left me
deep in the woods and promised they'd be back.
I'm the one who shoved a bent, withered, grandmother
into the flames. I've never forgotten her howls.
If you believe my father's tears
meant more to me than the rubies and pearls
I cast at his feet, think again.
They say forgiveness heals—
for me it was just a roof over my head.

LOVE AS INVASIVE SPECIES
ELLEN KOMBIYIL

CORNERSTONE PRESS, 2024
$21.95

BOOK REVIEW
ALEXANDER GAST

AT SEVEN, or eight, or some other similarly demarcated sector of those hazy, burnt-orange childhood years, my mother gave me a Rubik's Cube: a cruel gift, perhaps, for a brain like mine, having already displayed an incurable inability to comprehend algorithms, formulas, or any scrap of mathematical wherewithal essential to the solving of the thing. I twisted aimlessly. I watched patterns appear, then vanish, like shooting stars.

The experience was not unlike reading Ellen Kombiyil's *Love as Invasive Species,* which, though lacking a single, color-stratified solution like the one afforded to the Rubik's Cube, is ripe with sparkling versatility, shifting based on how the reader chooses to engage with the book. *Love* is a tête-bêche, or a "double-book," meaning, as suggested by the descriptor, that it comprises two books, intertwined. Each contains twenty poems. Holding the book at its A-Side, I read the book through to the middle, where the poem "To scribble down the bright magenta, begin again in the begot begun," oriented sideways on a two-page spread, bridges the gap between the first and second books. From here, *Love* flips 180. The back cover becomes the front cover; the front becomes the back, and the B-Side begins.

It clashes. It synergizes. Most remarkably, it transcends the double-book format and opens itself not just to two different readings, but to a near-infinite number. Read the first poem in the A-Side, then the first in B, or read companion poems together; for instance, read "Grade

School" (A.6), then follow its stated partner-poem to the second book with "Not About Sex" (B.15). Or, ditch all this and read it however you choose; *Love as Invasive Species* begs to be read in any way you wish to read it, and will reveal different secrets, different truths, depending. It only asks for your time and for your curiosity. I was happy to oblige.

Like all great poetry must, on some level, be, Kombiyil's poetry is preoccupied with life and death and the vast plains spanning the two. With "Prayer," the book begins – or ends, depending on your approach – in birth: "Here, / at the length-of-a-vein, / from navel's hollow to / how-low-the-azalea-bloom, / your propulsion into / the expectant room" (A.1), then, as in "Love Song with Contradictions," into aging, growing: "as a girl, when I first touched / myself, I thought *I'll die from this*" (A.5). Always there is death, looming: "even dead Aunt Blanche / at the dining table séance / predicted I'd get killed by a bus" ("Vixen Lessons") (A.8); "It was the time / of year when hatchlings // fell from / nests" ("Landscape with Waterfall and Ibises") (A.15); a tarantula, in the book's titular poem, "its carcass a dropped glove I'll bury in the yard / beside a house quietly erupting" ("Love as Invasive Species") (B.11-12). Remarkably, life is always close behind this death. Animals, humans are often buried in the collection, sprouting plants from the dirt: "The haphazard tulips I'd plant over her" ("Lament with Tulips and Crows") (B.25), "truth was a rose garden / sprouted on our wrists. / Our first cat we buried / out back" ("Days of 1988") (A.24), "The buried cat / sprouted a raspberry / bush" ("Birthday") (A.2).

The tête-bêche form proves fertile ground for these reflections on life and death. The living die, resurrect, and perish all over again, depending on the order in which you consume the poems. "Here we sit/sat," writes Kombiyil in "Dear Lost Beloved," blurring the lines between the past and the present, between the living and the dead (B.30). Images of death are sharp, foreboding, but are often grown with just enough room for life to trickle through.

At times inseparable from the themes of mortality are the ever-present evocations of generational inheritance. Side B begins with a chronology, which traces the poet's lineage back to her great-grandmother, born in 1897, and follows through to the present day. It is abundantly clear, through both the detail of the chronology and the book's shimmering ancestral poetry, that Kombiyil approaches the subject of familial legacy with a great deal of care. Always, this legacy simmers with quiet power. In "Lament with Trash Night and Slugs," the speaker's grandmother nears death and "scraped / at metal railings for anyone / who'd listen. Remember / who I am, she said" (A.33). *Love as Invasive Species* fulfills this wish. The book is an act of remembering, of keeping the dead alive.

The effects of mother on child, child upon mother, and the greater inter-generational helix of connection are powerful forces in the book. "O daughter," writes Kombiyil in "Freesia," "the knot of us – / how do I / unteach you this?" (B.34).

Love is also a meditation on fullness, on hunger. With "Prayer," Kombiyil wastes no time establishing hunger as a driving force in the book, writing, in its opening lines: "Daughter, if I forget to teach you / to hunger, to sup as I did" (A.1). We chase this same hunger throughout the tête-bêche. Cake, in the dark: "How sweet it was, / feasting like that / in the dark" ("Birthday") (A.3); or the birds in "Sugarfruit," "feasting branch to branch," while the family below relishes in "watermelon rinds / strewn in a dazzle of flies" (A.12); the "greasy pizza, cheap / baklava" of "Days of 1988" (A.24); a "ham & turkey sandwich," in "Love Song with Contradictions" (B.13); or, strangely, in "Hair," with the assertion that "The hair is like / peaches [...] / if you put it near / your mouth" (B.32). Hunger and fullness consume one another like ouroboros. Both are present nearly everywhere in the book, and much like life and death, the opposite forces amplify one another. "We were always falling // [...] our bodies pulsing with famine" ("Days of 1985") (A.23).

The result of all this cacophony, this symphony of contradiction and image-warring-image, image-wedding-image, is a strange, poignant, delicious book. It is part elegy, part frantic spell, cast to bring back the departed – much like the "old / Incantation" in "Black Fly Summer" (A.27). Above all else, though, it is a love song: for daughters, mothers, grandmas, and their mothers, and for the unseen, sprawling tower of ancestry. A love song for the scraps of beauty found in living as a part of something. For the "warmth-milk-blood," connecting "me-to-you" ("To scribble down the bright magenta, begin again in the begot begin") (A/B). ◆

"IN ANY EVENT" FROM LIFE ON EARTH
DORIANNE LAUX

W.W. NORTON, 2024
$26.99

A CLOSE READING
ROB GREENE

THE POEM "In Any Event" is most especially pertinent in these times. This poem is also one of my all-time favorites; therefore, I feel "In Any Event" warrants a close reading.

This poem's audience is open to all as the word choice is largely disyllabic and each line shines with each image, helping us feel better no matter how everything stands at this confusing time of regression. There is a lot more to be said for the divisions between high culture and low/pop culture, though poetry is neither and both at the same time because it overarches it all.

Those who seek to write the poem that will unite all people should not be discouraged, as that can be a useful muse to write to. "In Any Event" by Dorianne Laux is a poem that reaches beyond our fractures:

In Any Event

If we are fractured
we are fractured
like stars
bred to shine
in every direction,
through any dimension,
billions of years

since and hence.
I shall not lament
the human, not yet.
There is something
more to come,
our hearts
a gold mine
not yet plumbed,
an uncharted sea.
Nothing is gone forever.
If we came from dust
and will return to dust
then we can find our way
into anything.
What we are capable of
is not yet known,
and I praise us now,
in advance.

These lines morph the human race into the stars and hearts into gold from earth to space to sea to dust, offering readers the hope we so need right now. Here is an experience that is fully imagined because the poet, Dorianne Laux, is a keen observer who has experienced the elements that bind us. And she is, therefore, able to catch that which is most amiss. Thinking about the memorable line from the first celestial event of the film *Contact,* in which the protagonist states, "They should have sent a poet," I would want to send someone with Dorianne Laux's eye.

In "In Any Event," first published within the volume 9.2 issue of *Raleigh Review* in 2019, the themes that unite us are present in the constellations and in the sea. Laux's poem ventures that we are better than the current times and that we shall come out of this because,

If we came from dust ...
then we can find our way
into anything.
What we are capable of

is not yet known,
and so I praise us now,
in advance. ◆

Reference:

Greene, R. *The poetry school of experience.* Ph.D. Thesis at University of Birmingham 2020, England.

FROM THE PUBLISHER

OUR *Raleigh Review* is now lapping the sun fifteen times and counting.

There was some talk about linking *Raleigh Review* up with a local state university after our first issue was released. Instead of linking up with a Uni we rolled our organization off campus to a loft in the Five Points antique district of Raleigh. Our rent was affordable at that time, so we rolled with it for two years and had a blast serving the community at the height of the great recession. A number of characters, and some pretty odd propositions, came through our doors. When I heard rumors that our landlady said we were dealing in more than just magazines, books, and events, I immediately sent her our notice, and we swiftly ended that rental agreement with the full support of our Board of Directors.

We'd signed on to another much larger space that was in need of a lot of work and repairs. We took to it to get the space ready as we had Marie Howe flying in a few weeks later. That was quite an event and the community came out in droves for that *free* reading.

Shortly after three years of successful events, my preemie twins arrived three months early and that is the reason we changed gears, moving away from in-person events to focus entirely on the magazine. Things got tough at that point and there were many times we could have compromised our ethics, but still, we dug in, and we went virtual in 2014 before it was fashionable. We kept pushing forward to keep producing issue after issue for fifteen years now in all the right ways.

Our team, past and present, have been the very best friends and they have made my role as publisher to be so much fun and enjoyable. It is a lot of work that we all share. Some of our team members broke my heart when they had to depart our beloved magazine. Many have left due to expanding families, for the amazing *miracle of life,* and I must say, if I were not right here in Raleigh, I likely would have bailed as well when my twins were born way early. The team did allow me to take off nine months during that time, and I am very grateful to our team.

No one really can compete when it comes to those precious little ones.

And that brings me to our amazing Editor-in-Chief, Dr. Landon Houle, who has her priorities in order. We wish her and her family the very best in this joyous time as their family expands to include Little Baby Girl Houle! As with all who have to take a break for various reasons such as parenting (writers, artists, and poets do make the very best parents by the way) all are welcome to return whenever they wish. Our door is always open to those who put their families first.

We, with *Raleigh Review,* have done so well for much of the fifteen years without a physical space. That said, resilience, hard work, and know-how have helped us gain enough momentum to begin looking once again for a home for our *Raleigh Review,* and we are looking forward to making this happen.

I likely over-worry at times on what could happen with *Raleigh Review* after reaching a time when I can no longer run it and that is really none of my business. Answers to these questions are with our Board of Directors and our Team. I mean, as much as I take care in my role with the organization, *Raleigh Review* is not my only baby. When it comes down to it, this magazine belongs to everyone. That's one reason we went with the 501(c)(3) nonprofit status, to make this entity that is its own being. *Raleigh Review* is way bigger than any one individual.

Raleigh Review is now fifteen years old as of the 21st of February 2025, and *Raleigh Review* is not going anywhere anytime soon but we're weighing all of what could happen with the magazine when the current team can no longer continue. The important thing that we must remember is not to try to force anything. We must allow whatever will happen to happen organically without any undue pressure from any individual—including me, the founder. As we continue to produce one fine issue at a time, together, we thank you for reading. ◆

Rob Greene, publisher

contributors

LAUREN CAMP serves as New Mexico Poet Laureate. She is the author of eight poetry collections, most recently *In Old Sky* (Grand Canyon Conservancy, 2024), which grew out of her experience as Astronomer-in-Residence at Grand Canyon National Park. Her poems have been translated into Mandarin, Turkish, Spanish, French, and Arabic. www.laurencamp.com

CARLIN CORSINO is a North Carolina poet, Veteran, and emergency physician. He has been nominated for the Pushcart Prize on multiple occasions and has won several state-level poetry awards. Other recent work is forthcoming or featured in *3ELEMENTS* and *Door = Jar*.

KRISTIN EMANUEL holds an MFA in poetry from the University of Kansas, where she studied eco-fabulism and the comics poetry movement. Her latest poems, essays, and comics have appeared in *Ecotone, Blackbird,* and *The Rumpus.* You can find a list of her selected publications at: https://kristinemanuel.com/.

ALEXANDER GAST is the 2024-25 Publishing Intern at *Raleigh Review.* He studies creative writing at the University of North Carolina at Chapel Hill, where he is on a Thomas Wolfe scholarship. His poetry is featured or forthcoming in *Oyster River Pages, Ghost City Review,* and *Shooter Literary Magazine.* Gast is the editor of *The Fool's World* magazine.

ROB GREENE is the founder of *Raleigh Review,* and he is a father of four.

BREANNA GROW is a Central Illinois reporter turned Madison, Wisconsin poet and nonprofit sector jill of all trades. She can be found on the ground investigating bugs, mushrooms and other eye-catching life forms.

AUDREY HALL is a poet, literature scholar, and megafauna enthusiast from Mississippi. Her poems appear in *Alaska Quarterly Review, Okay Donkey, Atlanta Review, Texas Review Press's Southern Poetry Anthology,* and others. She reads for *Kitchen Table Quarterly.* In 2022, her poetry was nominated for a Best of the Net Award.

BETSY JOHNSON'S manuscripts have been finalists in the National Poetry Series Competition, the University of Wisconsin Poetry Prizes, and the Anhinga Prize for Poetry. Her work has appeared in *Iowa Review* (online), *Boulevard, Prairie Schooner,* and *Alaska Quarterly Review.*

PATRICK KINDIG is the author of the poetry collection *fascinations* (2025), the poetry chapbook *all the catholic gods* (2019), and the academic monograph *Fascination: Trance, Enchantment, and American Modernity* (2022). His poems have appeared in the *American Poetry Review, Colorado Review, Washington Square Review, Copper Nickel,* and other journals.

IAN LINDSAY is a current Ph.D. candidate at Georgia State and holds an MFA from the University of Central Florida. He is a fiction finalist for *Solstice*'s annual literary contest and the Steven R. Guthrie Memorial Writers' Festival Contest. As a first-generation Filipino American, he strives to find intersectionality and celebrate culture in writing. Ian also enjoys writing the dark and the strange. He is an assistant editor for *Five Points,* and his work can be read in *Pembroke, Variant Literature, Miracle Monocle, Pinyon,* and more.

NATHAN ALLING LONG grew up in a log cabin, worked on a queer commune, and now lives in Philadelphia. Their work appears in *Tin House, Master's Review, Electric Lit,* and *Best Small Fictions 2023. The Origin of Doubt,* their collection of fifty short fictions, was a 2019 Lambda Award finalist.

HILL RUSHING LUM enjoys long drives and a good cup of coffee. She currently lives with her family in New Mexico.

JEFF MCRAE is an employment specialist for disabled youth and young adults. He earned an MFA in Poetry from Washington University, St. Louis and an MA in Writing from the University of New Hampshire. New poems are forthcoming in *North Dakota Quarterly, Euphony Journal, Hiram Poetry Review, Antiphony,* and elsewhere.

STEVE NICKMAN'S poetry collection, *To Sleep with Bears,* is now available from Wordtech (2022). He is a psychiatrist who works mainly with kids, teenagers and young adults. He has a strong interest in the experiences and dilemmas of adoptees and their families and is working on a book about therapy, *The Wound and the Spark.* Steve's poetry has recently appeared in *Pleiades, Nimrod, Summerset Review, Tar River Review, Tule Review,* and *JuxtaProse.* He lives in Brookline, Massachusetts and is a member of Poemworks: The Workshop for Publishing Poets.

PATRICIA O'DONNELL is Professor Emerita in Creative Writing at the University of Maine at Farmington. Her work has appeared in *The New Yorker, Brevity, Agni Review,* and other places. Her books include a memoir, a collection of short fiction, and three novels, most recently *A Symmetry of Husbands.*

J. DOMINIC PATACSIL is a fiction writer hailing from Indiana. He is a graduate of the MFA program at the University of New Hampshire. His debut collection of stories, *Bald Spot,* will be published by Broken Tribe Press in 2025. Learn more at www.jdpatacsil.com.

VICTORIA JEAN REYNOLDS is a MFA candidate at George Mason University. Her work was most recently featured in *West Trade Review* and *Passengers Journal,* and forthcoming in *South Carolina Review, Santa Clara Review,* and *Salt Hill Journal.* She is the Poetry Editor for *phoebe* and *Stillhouse Press.* You can find her on Instagram at toreyntial.

LAURA ROSENTHAL holds an MFA in poetry from Pacific University and has published, or has poems forthcoming, *in Boog City, Buddhist Poetry Review, Driftwood Press, Chicago Quarterly Review,* and other journals. She leads workshops on writing and spiritual practice and is a member of the Community of Writers.

BRIANNA STEIDLE is a poet and translator and holds an MFA from The Writing Seminars at Johns Hopkins University. Her work has appeared or is forthcoming in *Poetry London, The Missouri Review, Plume, Boulevard,* and elsewhere.

BRENDAN STERMER is the author of the letterpress chapbook *Forgotten Frequencies* (NDSU Press, 2023) and the host of *Interesting People Reading Poetry,* a shortform podcast where artists and luminaries read a favorite poem and share what it means to them. He lives in East Grand Forks, Minnesota.

KATHERINE BARRETT SWETT is a retired teacher living in New York City. Her first collection, *Voice Message,* was selected by Erica Dawson for the 2019 Donald Justice Prize and was published by Autumn House Press in 2020.

SCOTT POMFRET is the author of Since *My Last Confession: A Gay Catholic Memoir; Hot Sauce: A Novel;* and over fifty stories published in, among others, *Ecotone, SmokeLong Quarterly, New Orleans Review,* and *Fiction International.* An MFA candidate at Emerson College, Scott's working on a comic queer Know-Nothing alternative history novel set in antebellum New Orleans. www.scottpomfret.com.

contributors cont.

KIMBERLY SUAZO is a Dominican American from the Bronx living in the Midwest. "The Alien" is her first published short story.

KEVIN THOMASON is the author of the poetry collection, *Even the Sky,* forthcoming this year by Cornerstone Press. He is from Memphis, Tennessee and teaches in the MFA program at McNeese State University.

ANGELA TOWNSEND is a four-time Pushcart Prize nominee and seven-time Best of the Net nominee. Her work appears or is forthcoming in *Arts & Letters, Chautauqua, Pleiades, SmokeLong,* and *West Trade Review.* She graduated from Princeton Seminary and Vassar and writes for a cat sanctuary. Her poet mother is her best friend.

EMILY WITHENBURY is a multi-disciplinary artist based in Virginia. She writes about the physical body as a map for our emotional landscapes. Previously, she danced professionally in San Francisco and owned a café/bakery in Massachusetts. Now, she is an MFA candidate at Hollins University where she hoards unpublished poetry.

LISA ZERKLE'S poems have appeared in *Quartet, Heavy Feather Review, The Collagist, Nimrod, storySouth, LEON Literary Review* and elsewhere. A graduate of the MFA Program for Writers at Warren Wilson College, she serves as an editor for *Painted Bride Quarterly* and a reader for *West Trade Review*/Iron Oak Editions.

Raleigh Review Turns